# ALWAYS
# THE BEST MAN

# ALWAYS
# THE BEST MAN

BY

FIONA HARPER

First published in Great Britain 2012 by Mills & Boon, an imprint of Harlequin (UK) Limited. Large Print edition 2012 Harlequin (UK) Limited, Eton House, 18-24 Paradise Road, Richmond, Surrey TW9 1SR

© Fiona Harper 2012

ISBN: 978 0 263 22629 4

Harlequin (UK) policy is to use papers that are natural, renewable and recyclable products and made from wood grown in sustainable forests. The logging and manufacturing process conform to the legal environmental regulations of the country of origin.

Printed and bound in Great Britain by CPI Antony Rowe, Chippenham, Wiltshire

For Dad, who likes sailing
much better than he likes reading romance. x

# CHAPTER ONE

IF DAMIEN STONE had been a woman, he'd have become a bit of a standing joke by now. Three times a bridesmaid was unlucky, apparently. Double that number would have knelled the bells of matrimonial doom. Clucking aunts would have reminded him of that at every opportunity, told him to get a move on before he was left on the shelf.

But no one had ever made the mistake of thinking Damien was a girl, and he hadn't been a bridesmaid once, thankfully. Nobody seemed to mind he'd been a best man so many times. If anything, other men clapped him on the back and congratulated him for such an accomplishment. No, Damien didn't think there was anything unlucky about it.

It meant his friends respected him, thought him a stalwart ally. It took a certain kind of person to stand beside a friend at the front of a church, as that man prepared to utter the most life-altering words of his existence. Someone who was reliable, who knew how to get things done. Someone with a little dignity. He supposed he should be flattered.

But more than that, he was thankful—because he was going to need to draw on all of that experience if he was going to survive this day.

Six times now he'd worn a buttonhole as he stood beside a good friend. Six times he'd stood at the front of a pretty stone church in the hush just before the bride made her entrance. But never before had his palms been so sweaty or his heart run around inside his ribcage like a wind-up toy gone mad.

However, never before had the woman of his dreams been standing at the doors of the church, about to make her way down the aisle towards him.

He turned and looked at Luke, his best friend, and Luke gave him a fortifying smile and clapped him on the back. Damien swallowed. He was glad it was Luke standing here beside him. He didn't think he could have made it through the day if it had been anyone else.

He tried to smile, but a nerve in his cheek made his lip twitch. Humour flashed in Luke's eyes and

Damien thought his friend was about to make one of his usual wry remarks, but just at that moment there was a ripple of movement behind them. Row upon row of heads turned towards the back of the church, like some nuptial Mexican wave, and the organ began to play.

He couldn't look back at first, had to prepare himself for what he was about to see. This was it. No turning back after this. The future would be set in stone.

It was only when Luke nudged him in the ribs that he sucked in a stealthy breath through his nostrils then looked over his shoulder.

She was perfect.

He didn't really look at the dress. Just her.

But then Sara Mortimer always had been pretty wonderful in his eyes. He'd thought so from the day he'd seen her across the room at a crowded bar, laughing with Luke, and had felt as if he'd been hit by a truck. Side on.

After today the rest of the world would be left in no doubt about her perfection, either. The white satin dress was pure class, and her soft blonde hair had been caught up in a twist of some kind behind her head. She wore a veil and a simple tiara and held a bunch of lilies, tied together with a thick white ribbon.

Sara was poised and elegant, intelligent, kind. He couldn't find one fault with her—apart from her taste in men, maybe.

He let go of the breath he'd been holding and grabbed another while he had the chance.

It seemed to take ages for the bridesmaids to waft past in a cloud of dull gold. Well, *most* of them wafted. The maid of honour had too much of a wiggle in her step to do anything as graceful as waft.

It wasn't just Sara's taste in men that let her down, then. Damien had never really understood why Sara was friends with Zoe. Another one of the bride's glowing qualities to add to his list, he supposed.

Where Sara was slender and cool and sophisticated, Zoe was too…everything. Not in the same class—and that didn't refer to her parents' wage brackets. Damien wasn't a snob. No, Zoe was too loud, too uninhibited. Too busting out of her bodice, if his eyes served him right. Was it even legal to have that much cleavage in a bridesmaid's dress?

For some bizarre reason, just her presence jarred

his senses and irritated him. Or was that just the
eye-watering perfume? She caught him looking
at her and her expression took on a saucy glimmer. She *knew* she got under his skin. Couldn't
she have left it alone for just one day? And today
of all days? He was sure she did…whatever she
did…on purpose, just to goad him.

And now Sara was almost at the front and he'd
been distracted, which only served to exasperate
him further.

Thankfully, at that moment the last of the
bridesmaids peeled away, leaving him with a vision of only Sara. He forgot instantly about bulging necklines, saucy glimmers and ginger curls
popping out of their grips. In comparison, Sara
was like a cool stream on a hot summer's day.
As she approached, she even gave him the small-
est and softest of smiles. Sadly, he didn't manage to return it; that nerve in his cheek had gone
into overdrive. For a moment, though, their eyes
connected and something flashed between them.
Something bittersweet he was sure would haunt
him on restless nights for years to come.

Because then Sara's gaze was on the man standing next to him, and her father placed her hand in
Luke's and stepped away. Now it was Damien's

turn to be forgotten, to be totally pushed out of someone else's mind by another.

The bride and groom stepped forward, eagerly looking at the minister. All eyes were on Sara and Luke, the happy couple, but all Damien could do was close his lids for a second, let his fingers close around the ring in his pocket.

Luke's ring. For Sara.

No, if it had been anyone else, he couldn't have made it through today. He couldn't have stood there and watched Sara marry anyone but Luke. He equally couldn't have refused when Luke had asked him to be his best man. Luke would have wanted to know why, and if there was one thing Damien was determined about it was that neither Luke nor Sarah would ever find out about his feelings for her, how they'd grown in strength, side by side with Luke's, as he'd fallen for his best friend's girlfriend.

He'd hidden those feelings successfully for the last eighteen months and he wasn't going to slip up now. No, Luke would never know. Even if it killed Damien to make sure of that.

Today of all days, Damien Stone needed to be the perfect best man.

* * *

As the congregation mumbled their way through 'Love Divine, All Loves Excelling', almost completely drowned out by the rabidly enthusiastic organist, Sara's cousin Tilly poked Zoe in the ribs with the stalky end of her bouquet.

Okay, maybe 'poked in the ribs' was a bit of an exaggeration. There was a bit too much *squish* where floristry met torso to accurately describe it as contact with bone. Zoe tried to ignore her, but Tilly leaned forward and whispered behind her lilies.

'Best man's hot,' she said, sneaking a glance across the aisle. 'Lucky you. As chief bridesmaid, you get first dibs.'

Zoe couldn't help glancing across at the man in question. How did he do that? Manage to look all grave and heartfelt as he sang, while other people just buried their noses behind their Order of Service and hit a few right notes in the chorus?

'If you like that sort of thing,' she mumbled back to Tilly.

If you liked tall, dark and handsome. If you liked long legs and good bone structure and that irritating sense of aloofness. Even now, with his mouth wide open, singing one of the long notes of the hymn, he looked good. Untouchable. And

Zoe had never been interested in anything that was too good to be touched, one step removed from life, as if it was something behind glass on display in a museum. Life was for getting your hands dirty, for jumping in one hundred per cent.

'What?' hissed Tilly, forgetting to shield her mouth with her bouquet. She earned herself a stern look from the mother of the bride. A woman who managed to scare the pants off the normally irrepressible Zoe St James. If, as the old wives' tale threatened, Sara was going to age into a gorgon like that, she'd have to find herself a new best friend once she hit forty.

'Are you blind?' Tilly added, ignoring her aunt's stare. Obviously the black sheep of the Mortimer family—which, funnily enough, put her a few notches higher in Zoe's opinion.

Zoe just rolled her eyes and shook her head ever so slightly. It was still enough motion, however, to send yet another curly tendril tumbling over her face. She was about to blow it out of her way when she caught the Gorgon's eye, and resorted to delicately tucking it behind her ear while the other woman's eyes narrowed.

She looked away, and her gaze was drawn inexplicably to the subject of their discussion.

No, not blind. Just not stupid.

She knew he couldn't stand the sight of her. Oh, he tried to hide it, and he actually did it rather well, but she'd been on the receiving end of similar treatment ever since she'd been old enough to open her mouth to recognise disapproval when she saw it.

Disdain. That was the word.

And that *disdainful* glimmer in Mr Perfect's eye when he glanced her way just made her want to deliberately provoke him. And Zoe wasn't one for resisting an urge whenever it hit. Life was too short. Just once she'd like to see him lose his cool, to see fire in those pale blue eyes instead of ice. In the past she'd got close a few times, but close wasn't good enough. What Zoe really wanted to see was the whole firework display.

Not today, unfortunately. She wouldn't do anything to upset Sara, and the poor deluded girl thought Mr Damien Stone was wonderful. Not as wonderful as the lovely Luke, obviously, but Zoe reckoned he came a close second in Sara's eyes. She turned to Tilly and made a silent gagging motion, to show just what she thought of her fellow bridesmaid's suggestion.

Whoops! The Gorgon was staring at them

openly now, her mouth thinning. And Zoe really didn't want to see tiny snakes popping up all over her head and burrowing their way up through the stiff and elaborate dove-grey hat. She turned to face the happy couple again, clutched her bouquet and started singing sweetly.

Mr Perfect must've caught the sudden motion out of the corner of his eye, because his head turned slightly and he glanced across. Zoe ignored him. Ignored the flicker she saw in those eyes before it was quickly hidden again. She put on her best angelic face and sang loudly, all the while warmed by the imagination that she could hear Damien Stone's blood hissing faintly as it boiled in his veins.

Oh, how she wanted to see that firework display.

But not tonight, Zoe. Keep a lid on it. Sara and Luke had decided they didn't want fireworks at the end of the reception, saying that everyone did it now and it seemed a bit of a cliché, so she guessed they wouldn't welcome a similar display of the interpersonal kind. Damien Stone's fuse would have to go unlit—for now.

But that didn't mean she couldn't mess with his head a little, did it?

\* \* \*

'Aren't you going to eat that?'

Damien stared at his half-finished individual pavlova for a second. He remembered taking a bite, but he didn't remember pushing it around his plate so much it had disintegrated into Eton Mess. He flexed his shoulder muscles slightly. His morning suit jacket felt as if it were shrinking.

'What's wrong with yours?'

He turned to look at the maid of honour sitting next to him at the top table. Ridiculous seating plan. He'd never been sat next to the maid of honour before, not in six other weddings.

'Nothing,' she replied sweetly. Too sweetly. 'It was stupendous…but rather small. That's why I want yours if you're not going to do it justice.'

Damien glowered at his plate briefly, as if the ravaged dessert somehow held some of the blame in this situation, and then shoved the plate in her direction, nobly resisting the urge to say anything about overfilled bodices.

'Knock yourself out.'

'Thanks.'

She dug in straight away, he noticed. Somehow that irritated him. He focused on a rather ugly pink hat somewhere else in the massive marquee and tried to will the minutes to go faster. Only a short time now and his official duties would be over. Soon he'd be able to slink off and find a good single malt to lubricate his petrified facial muscles. They'd set into a stupefied smile earlier in the day. Right about the time Sara had said, 'I do.'

Always the best man…

It was starting to sound like a joke to Damien now—and not a very funny one. While he enjoyed helping his friends out in this way, he was beginning to feel like the odd one out. So many of his friends were all settled down and happy now, just as he wanted to be. Damien felt as if he was the unlucky jockey in a horse race, whose starting gate had failed to open while all the other riders were racing away from him. And now his best friend had snapped up the one woman Damien had considered a viable candidate for being Mrs Stone, it was even more disheartening.

'Mmm. You don't know what you're missing,' Zoe murmured next to him.

Damien braced his aching shoulders to stop them sagging. Unfortunately, he knew *exactly* what he was losing out on today. How could he not when she was sitting only three places away? He made the mistake of glancing to his right, the opposite direction from the pavlova-devouring machine on his left.

He must have momentarily forgotten the granite smile, because he snagged Sara's attention for a second. She made the most adorable face, asking him what was wrong by pulling her lips down and creasing her forehead into a little frown.

He shook his head, shrugged one shoulder and resurrected the ghoulish grin he'd been fooling everybody with all day. Blast that Zoe. Her dessert stealing had made him lose focus. Why couldn't he have been seated next to Sara's mum? He could have distracted himself from this train wreck of an afternoon by charming her socks off.

Sara noted his changed expression and gave him a soft smile before turning her attention back to her new husband.

Damien wanted to sigh, but his ribs were too tight under his skin to allow his lungs to expand that fully, so he made up for it by huffing out an exasperated little snort through his nose.

'Calm down, tiger.' The words were slightly muffled through a layer of whipped cream and raspberry coulis. 'There's still a bit left if you're regretting your generosity.'

He turned to look at Zoe as she nudged the almost empty plate his way. A lump of soggy meringue with a single berry on top was all that remained. Her mouth was pressed together in a knowing little smile and her eyes glittered with unsaid words.

Regretting your generosity *to me*, they seemed to be saying.

He shook his head, not trusting his tongue to remain civil.

'Sure?' she asked, as she began to move her spoon into position to capture the last morsel. 'I'm sure I could pilfer one for you from somewhere, or sweet-talk one of the waiters...'

'I'm sure you could,' Damien replied dryly.

That saucy glint again. Now his suit was three sizes too small instead of two. And all that shrinkage was making him feel hot and jittery.

'Oh, well,' she said and popped the now full spoon into her mouth, turning it upside down at the last moment so she could suck every square millimetre of the silver clean. She closed her eyes and murmured her appreciation deep down in her throat.

Damien experienced a quick, hot jolt of something unexpected. Something he didn't really want to identify. Especially when it was prompted by Zoe St James's mobile lips sliding along a spoon.

Thankfully, Sara's father chose that moment to stand up and clink his dessert fork against his glass. All heads turned towards the top table and Damien instantly sat up straighter and put his game face back on.

In fact, he was so busy making sure he wasn't giving off any unwanted non-verbal cues to more than a hundred guests that he didn't even hear the opening sentences of Colin's speech. He couldn't let anything slip. Not a facial twitch, not a glance in the wrong direction. No one must guess that he was anything less than the perfect best man. But all the while the guilt, the frustration, the slow, glowing flicker of rage kept building inside him until he wished he had a giant version of the metal cages that went round champagne corks. If he wasn't very much mistaken, his head was about to explode from his shoulders, and that wouldn't do before the toasts were over.

More words. They floated past like yachts in a stiff breeze. Words he'd heard a hundred times before at occasions like this. Until the end of the speech, that was…

'So…' Colin Mortimer beamed at his wife and

then his daughter '…Brenda and I decided we wanted to do something special for our little girl.' He paused for dramatic effect as his only daughter smiled back up at him. 'We know you'd planned a simple honeymoon sailing Luke's pride and joy down the south coast, but we decided we'd like to upgrade you a little…'

Damien sat up straighter. Uh-oh. Luke had planned the perfect honeymoon for himself and Sara, one Damien would have given his right arm to have. A fortnight on *Dream Weaver* with no one but Sara? It sounded like heaven. Oh, Luke would smile and thank his new father-in-law if he produced tickets for an all-inclusive break in some slick hotel, but his dream holiday would be ruined.

Always the one to take charge, to make sure all the details were ironed out and perfect, Damien started composing a speech in his head, one he'd have with Colin afterwards, to try and help Luke back graciously out of this latest development.

The father of the bride handed Luke a wallet. 'Two plane tickets to the Virgin Islands—'

Damien began rehearsing that little speech in earnest.

'—and the use of a luxury yacht for three weeks!'

There was a collective gasp from the guests and then people started to clap and cheer. Damien was frozen. For some reason he couldn't move. Hell, he couldn't even think straight.

Sara was hugging her father and Luke was pumping his hand enthusiastically.

No wonder. Luke had dreamed of sailing those turquoise Caribbean waters since he and Damien had both been racing little Laser dinghies together at summer sailing school. However, since Sara had put her foot down about a transatlantic crossing for a honeymoon, Luke had had to settle for West Country cruising instead.

Why hadn't Damien thought of doing this for them? He should have done. After all, it was sailing that had bonded him and Luke as friends all those years ago.

*You know why.*

Damien closed his eyes. Yes, he did know. He'd let his guilt at having feelings for his best friend's woman cloud everything.

*And the jealousy too. Don't forget the jealousy.*

No. I tried so hard not to let that happen. I don't

want anything but the best for them. At least, I don't *want* to want anything but the best for them.

But he had been jealous. As much as he'd tried to outrun it, he had.

And it made him lower than pond life. Which was why, when one hundred and fifteen guests rose and joined Colin Mortimer in toasting the happy couple, Damien began to shake. Not on the surface—he was too well-practised at being the textbook best man for that—but deep down in his gut. He was almost surprised the untouched champagne glass in his hand didn't rattle.

And then the father of the bride turned to him, a beneficent smile on his face, nodded and sat down.

Damien rose, his legs propelling him upwards suddenly so he hit his thighs against the table top and made the silverware jiggle.

His turn now. His turn to spout and toast—and lie. He swallowed, knowing he was about to open his mouth and prove himself the biggest hypocrite in the world.

# CHAPTER TWO

THE whole room went quiet. Zoe felt a familiar and almost irresistible urge to blurt something shocking out, just to inject some life into the dead and faultless silence. Instead she rested one elbow on the table and twisted her head round to hear His Highness say something pompous.

Only he didn't say anything. Pompous or otherwise. He just stood there, staring at everyone. The only movement was a Jurassic Park-type mini-tremor in his glass of champagne.

He opened his mouth. A few wedding guests leaned forward. Damien Stone was famous for his best man speeches. People joked about crashing weddings just to hear them. He closed his lips again.

The silence began to get awkward. Children began to fidget.

Damien Stone cleared his throat.

Zoe seriously considered jumping up and shouting, *Knickers*!

But just in the nick of time a noise came from the back of his mouth, so quiet she was probably the only person who heard it. But she saw him tense, push the sound forward until it grew and words followed it.

'I haven't got anything clever to say.'

People began to look at each other and smile. They knew this was just the start. It would be clever and funny and touching. It would.

He took a deep breath. 'Just that Luke and Sara are truly the perfect couple.'

Zoe frowned. She'd been all revved up to smirk inwardly at his artfully crafted spiel, but his simple sincerity had stolen all her thunder.

'And I can't do anything more than say that Luke is the best friend a man could have, and remind him he is the luckiest man in the world to have found Sara, and wish them a lifetime of happiness together.'

He paused, raised his glass to the bride and groom.

Zoe held her champagne flute up, but her eyes were on the best man. Had that really been a catch in his voice when he'd said his best friend's name?

'To Luke and Sara,' he said simply, and sud-

denly the whole marquee was on its feet, clapping
and cheering and marvelling at how, once again,
the best man had outdone himself.

Damien knocked back his fizz and sat down,
exhaling heavily. If Zoe hadn't known any better
she'd have thought he was nervous. But that would
have meant he was feeling an emotion other than
smug superiority, which was clearly impossible.

She took a sip of her own drink and sat down
beside him. Now, she'd never been one to want
to cause Damien Stone's head to swell any bigger, but for some reason she felt she needed to
say something, to tell him how perfect his words
had been.

'That was—'

His head snapped round in surprise—as if he'd
totally forgotten she existed and had been occupy-
ing the space beside him—and he fixed her with
those cold blue eyes.

His voice was low and hoarse. 'Just don't, Zoe.
Not right now.'

'But I wasn't going to—'

The glare he gave her made her shut her mouth
abruptly. And if he hadn't been concentrating
on being just so fierce and condescending, he

might have realised what a miraculous feat that had been.

And then, while all eyes were on the bride and groom, while the happiness seemed to be spilling out of the other guests and pooling around their feet, Damien rose stiffly from his chair and headed out into the twilight.

Zoe sat back in her gold-sprayed, velvet-seated chair and crossed her arms. Not even good enough to offer the precious Damien Stone a few words of congratulation. She had obviously sunk to a new low in his eyes. But Zoe didn't let that cold feeling settle deep down inside like it wanted to. She couldn't. She'd promised herself that never again would a man like that make her feel this way. And if crumbling in defeat wasn't an option, she had no alternative but to go the other way. So, by his actions, the best man had decreed tonight would be all-out war, and the evening reception would be their battlefield.

Look out, Damien Stone, because all those snotty comments you've ever dished out are coming back to bite you on that finely toned rear end. Tonight, Karma is wearing a bridesmaid's dress—and she's in one hell of a mood.

* * *

'Those ballroom dancing lessons really paid off in the end.'

Zoe smiled into the face of the man who had just twirled her into his arms. He really was looking particularly handsome today. And so he should.

'I beg to differ, Luke. You've trodden on my foot twice already, and we both know why.'

He gazed above her shoulder, looking every inch the dashing groom. 'I have no idea what you're talking about.'

At that point Zoe did a little bit of toe-crunching of her own. 'Really?' she said innocently. 'And there was me thinking all those last-minute work emergencies on a Thursday night were merely a ruse so you could cry off and go down the pub with your mates.'

Luke's smile spread wider. 'No,' he said. 'Still no idea. You must have the wrong person.'

The smile wavered momentarily, however, when he misjudged a step and almost sent the pair of them flying. Thankfully, Zoe rescued them with quick thinking and even quicker feet. There was a reason for that, too.

'You owe me,' she whispered in his ear as she clutched onto his sleeves. 'You knew Sara wouldn't want to go to those lessons on her own. You knew she'd drag me along as a substitute.'

Luke just beamed as if he was on a TV ballroom dancing contest, fixing his eyes beyond her. 'And just look how well you can waltz now,' he said. 'You have me to thank for that.'

Zoe wanted to punch him. Or tickle him. She wasn't sure which.

Luke saved himself by having the decency to look just a little repentant. 'Okay, I do owe you. And I've just had an idea for a very fitting peace offering…'

He paused while he concentrated on changing direction so they didn't plough into the four-tiered cake.

'I know that all the wedding craziness has meant that you haven't had the chance to have a proper holiday this year.'

He *should* know that, Zoe thought. She'd moaned long and hard about it often enough.

'Well, *Dream Weaver*, thanks to the generosity of my new father-in-law, is now going to be sitting idle and unloved at her mooring for the next two weeks. Why don't you make use of her?'

Zoe laughed so hard that the couple next to them

lost their timing. 'Don't be daft, Luke! I don't know the first thing about sailing.'

'From what I remember, the few times you have made it on board, the highlights were sunbathing on the deck and sipping wine in the cockpit while the stars came out.'

Well, there was that. It had all been *awfully* civilised. And she could almost imagine herself using the twenty-year-old yacht as a base for a relaxing holiday. She could explore the surrounding countryside and the nearby village of Lower Hadwell, wander down narrow streets lined with ice cream-coloured houses. She started to dream of long pub lunches and enough time to read the stack of paperbacks that had been gathering dust on her bedside table.

She must have looked as if she were weakening because Luke added, 'I can always arrange for my friend Matthew to take you out on a couple of day trips—up and down the river, or round to one of the little beaches near the estuary that can only be reached by boat.'

Zoe stopped turning and looked Luke straight in the eye. 'Matthew? The Matthew who has the shaggy blond hair and the cute, tight little rounded—'

Luke burst out laughing.

She half-closed her eyelids. 'I was going to say "nose".'

'Of course you were. But, yes, *that* Matthew.'

Well, that sounded like the perfect recipe for a last-minute, spontaneous holiday. Fit, toned surfer-dudes and throwing things into a suitcase were definitely her thing. She instantly forgave Luke for the further three times he would tread on her feet before the dance was over.

'In that case,' she said, dipping low as Luke very bravely swung her into a pose, 'you might just have a deal.'

The music changed to a slow, sweeping tune, but Damien hardly noticed it. He was tired. Bone-deep, soul-weary exhausted. Which was odd, because if anyone should have built up a best man brand of stamina by now, it should have been him.

He checked his watch. Nine-thirty.

It couldn't be long now before Sara and Luke left the grounds of this smart country house hotel to begin a new life together. And once the car had disappeared, even while the tin cans were still clattering down the drive, he planned to slip away.

He had a room booked at the hotel, but he wasn't

going to use it. He needed to go back to his flat, be by himself, not extend the aftermath of the wedding with nightcaps with the other guests or jolly communal breakfasts the next morning.

Just before he looked up from his watch he became aware of someone standing in front of him. A quick glance downwards revealed his worst fear—white satin and a pair of matching shoes.

'Come on, you...' Sara said in that gentle, clear voice of hers. Damien transferred his gaze to his brogues. She was too close. If he looked up now, really let her see into his eyes, she might guess.

Slim fingers tugged at his jacket sleeve. 'We can't have you moping about in the corner on your own. You've got your pick of the bridesmaids, you know. Once upon a time that would have excited you.'

He looked up without actually looking *at* her, and shook his head. Why settle for second best?

'Well, you'll have to make do with me, then. Dance with me, Damien?'

He pulled air in through his nostrils and pushed it out again through his teeth. He stood up, unable to refuse this bride anything. Besides, she would think it odd if he refused, would probably send Luke to wheedle the secret he could never tell out of him.

Sara grasped his hand and pulled him towards the dance floor. So much for *slipping away.*

When she stopped, turned and waited for him to take her in his arms he almost bolted, but instead he stoically took her hand in his and drew her close. Not too close, however.

Imagine it's someone else, he told himself.

And it seemed to work, because they started to move their feet and he still felt relatively normal. There were no fireworks where they touched, no unexpected jolts or hot flushes. This was good. He had things under control.

'You've been fabulous today,' Sara said as he led her round the dance floor. 'Perfect.'

Damien smiled. A smile of duty. 'It was easy to do this for Luke,' he said. His words were plain, slightly evasive, but not devoid of truth. It *had* been easy to decide to support his best friend all the way when Luke had announced—in his own words—that he was going to marry the most wonderful woman in the world. Damien couldn't have done anything else. It wasn't in his bones.

But where the spirit was willing, the flesh had been weak. He hadn't been able to eradicate the growing feelings for the woman he was now holding in his arms. He'd tried. God, he'd tried.

Sara attempted to chat as they danced, but her efforts clanged off him and fell to the floor between their feet. He'd always been able to jest and banter with Sara before now, but after the emotional marathon he'd run today he found himself searching frantically for something to say.

Conversation would be good, Damien! Conversation would distract him from the feel of her waist beneath his fingers, the light touch of her hand on his shoulder, the rose-scented perfume that was flooding his nostrils and drowning his lungs.

He looked down, breaking eye contact. 'Your ring is beautiful,' he said.

Sara lifted her hand off his shoulder to inspect it, twisting her hand one way then the other. 'Yes, it is, isn't it?'

Damien looked at the elegant curve of white gold studded with diamonds that was wrapped around Sara's fourth finger. It suited her perfectly.

She smiled wide and replaced her hand on his shoulder. 'Zoe really outdid herself this time.'

'Zoe made *that*?'

He must have blurted that out in a rather uncharacteristic fashion because Sara burst out laughing and nodded. Damien looked again at the shiny, pale ring against the charcoal of his morning suit jacket, not quite able to get his head round what Sara had just told him.

He knew Sara and her girlfriends went wild for Zoe's jewellery but, from what he remembered of her pieces, they were chunky, asymmetric things, involving not just stones and settings, but shells or wooden beads or feathers. Sometimes all three. To be honest, he didn't get it. Must be a girl thing. He had always thought the simple chain and diamond pendant that Sara always wore was much more classy.

He felt a tap on his right shoulder. 'I think you owe me a dance,' a deep voice said. He twisted his head to find Luke grinning at his new bride, Zoe in his arms. Sara let her hands slide from Damien's shoulder and back as Luke moved towards them.

Let go, Damien told himself. It's time to let go…

It felt as if he had to peel himself from her.

'Not *her*,' Luke said, nodding towards his wife. 'I meant *you*, my fine figure of a man.'

They all laughed at the joke, the way Luke held his arms aloft in invitation to Damien, before using them to scoop Sara closer so he could nuzzle into her neck. And off they went like that, joined from forehead to toe.

That left Zoe and Damien without partners and staring at each other.

He knew what the polite thing to do was. Problem was that, right at this moment, he wasn't feeling particularly polite. He hesitated a fraction of a second too long, though, and one of Zoe's mobile eyebrows twitched in recognition of his predicament. A wry smile pressed her lips together. Not an expression of humour, but of challenge.

Damien recovered quickly and held out his arms, just as Luke had done a moment earlier, as if that tiny transaction had not just occurred between him and the maid of honour. Pretend it's all fine. Bury the uncomfortable feeling. That was what normally worked.

Zoe stepped into his hold, but the naughty twinkle in her eye told him her memory would not be so easy to erase. It also told him she would make him pay. Thankfully, the song was almost over.

But, as they started to move, the band segued into another tune, something in a four-four time with a bit of a Latin beat. He could hardly pull away now, thank her politely and head for the fresh night air outside the marquee, could he?

Damien growled inwardly. Now he had a whole song to get through. With a woman who—for no apparent reason—had not only decided she didn't like him, but had made it her mission in life to wind him up.

What a perfect way to end the evening.

Pompous ass, Zoe thought to herself, grinding her teeth gently as she held her smile in place. She'd show him.

You'd think, on a day like today, when they were both here to support their best friends, he could have let up a little. But, no, Mr Holier-than-thou Stone had to ramp up the superiority factor even further.

Well, thanks to all those ballroom dancing lessons Luke had skipped out on, Zoe knew how to rumba just fine. At least on the dance floor she'd show him who was top dog.

Despite the urge to clench all her muscles ready for a killer right hook, she made herself breathe out, concentrated on relaxing into the rhythm so her hips and waist twisted and flowed. The brides-maid's dress was perfect for it. Sara had chosen well. Satin, the colour of old gold, skimmed her hips and flared from her knees in a bias-cut skirt, and it moved sensuously with every step.

They danced in silence, but after a particularly tricky bit of footwork she glanced up at Damien to find him staring down hard at her.

'I thought the man was supposed to lead,' he said, his voice expressionless.

Zoe shrugged. 'This is a rumba. I'm just dancing the steps. Not my problem if it's beyond you.'

His grip on her hand tightened and he pulled himself up straight, bringing their bodies closer together. Zoe feigned nonchalance.

'Whoever said it was beyond me?'

Damien continued to stare at her, a slightly devilish smile kinking the side of his mouth, and his feet began to move in a pattern that had become horribly familiar to Zoe over the last couple of months. Rumba steps. Oh, hell. Of course Mr Perfect would be able to do this. Just another superpower to add to his vast collection.

At first they moved mechanically, stiffly, but as the song continued they both seemed to melt into the rhythm. None of those peacock-like, ostentatious moves from a ballroom competition for Damien Stone. His movements were slow, measured, restrained yet fluid—a style born more of the streets of Havana than from Gertrude Glitz's Ballroom Academy. Zoe adjusted her moves to match, no flinging arms or swinging feet; just the feeling of the teasing, back and forth rhythm snaking up from her core and moving her limbs.

She'd been so lost in the sways and pauses, the feeling that her muscles were turning to marshmallow, that it took a few moments to realise their gazes were still locked. His smile had gone now, replaced by a look of concentration that was at once unnerving and—dare she admit it?—sexy.

She swallowed. Her mouth had suddenly gone very, very dry.

They were closer now too, and she wasn't quite sure how they'd got that way, their torsos a hair's breadth from touching.

The bridesmaid's dress, which had been a little on the snug side up top already—thanks to a failed pre-wedding diet—now seemed to compress her ribs, making it hard to do anything but grab oxygen in short bursts.

No, no, no.

She was not going to forget just how up his own...backside...Damien Stone was just because he knew how to rumba, just because the slow

swaying, the leashed feeling of power in his movements, made her think about *other* superpowers
he might have.

Men like him were trouble. They said they liked
girls like her. They might even believe it when
they promised that quirkiness and a unique take
on life were enchanting, but sooner or later they
changed their minds.

She couldn't let this lazy rhythm lull her into a
stupor and forget all of that. In fact, she needed to
do the opposite. Men like Damien Stone needed
to be reminded that, actually, they *weren't* God's
gift, and that maybe they should climb down from
their impossibly high horses now and again and
remember that they were just like everyone else:
flawed, clueless…human. That was all she was
asking for. Surely that wasn't too much?

He must have a weakness, this man. His own
personal brand of kryptonite. She just had to find
out what that was—and then use it against him.

# CHAPTER THREE

DAMIEN felt the muscles of Zoe's torso tense quite clearly, even though his fingertips were only lightly resting on her shoulder blade, and it pulled him out of whatever delightful bubble he'd lost himself in. For a moment he'd been totally focused on the dancing, neither regretting the past—of what might have been had he met Sara first—or yearning for a future that would never be his. How odd, that it was with this woman he'd found a sense of calm in this nightmare of a day.

No more, though. The unusual softness that had been in Zoe's eyes was gone, replaced with the more familiar hard, cheeky, taunting one, and he mentally kicked himself for forgetting he was dancing with an unexploded bomb.

'I'm impressed,' she said, but the look in her eyes told him this compliment had a sting in its tail. 'I didn't think a man like you would be any good at something like this.'

Ouch. There it was. But gentler and more skilful than he'd expected.

A man like him. What was so wrong with that?

He found he couldn't let her remark go unchallenged. Dancing had been a good momentary distraction, but now she'd ruined that he'd resort to a bit of one-upmanship with Zoe, if that was what she wanted.

'A man like what?' he said through his teeth, still smiling, as he flicked his wrist and spun her out to the side.

She didn't miss a step, her hips moving like molasses, accentuated by the clinging fabric of her bridesmaid's dress.

'Oh, you know...' Her voice was light and breezy. 'Uptight. Buttoned-up.'

He ignored the comment, even though he noticed the movements of his torso became less fluid with each step, despite his efforts to the contrary. He bunched his shoulders, one after the other, and let them drop again. 'I'm not uptight.'

Zoe didn't answer—not with words—but her smile hitched to one side, giving her an impish air.

*Oh, no?* the smile said.

Damien shook his head, narrowing his eyes. And he *made* his lower half move more freely, just to prove her wrong. It wasn't quite the same as when he'd been truly relaxed a few moments before, but it was better than nothing, and he threw in a few dips and turns, just to keep her from noticing the difference.

She kept up, of course, adding her own brand of spice to each shift of weight, each wiggle. Grudgingly, he gave her silent credit.

But Damien didn't want to notice just how easy it was to dance with Zoe St James, didn't want to admit they complemented each other in any way at all, despite the growing sense of heat travelling up his body or the skipping of his pulse in his veins, so he tore his gaze away from hers, looked beyond her shoulder.

And instantly regretted it.

Without wanting to, he sought out the bride and groom on the crowded dance floor. They'd finished with any pretence of doing proper steps now and just clung to each other, her head resting on his shoulder, eyes closed in a state of bliss. A horrible emptiness settled on Damien.

Since his partner was probably the lesser of two evils, he switched his gaze to her and found her studying him. Without letting him lead, she released his hand, stepped out, free arm raised, and then moved back in again, coming close. Much too close.

Sara would never have danced with him like this, not even if they'd been a couple. And suddenly he was angry with Zoe for causing him to make comparisons, for making him notice who she *wasn't*, because that ache was growing now, filling his chest, catching his breath.

No, this wasn't Sara. She would never be Sara. And, on some entirely primal—and completely unreasonable—level, he wanted to make her pay for that.

He caught her in a ballroom hold, using slightly more pressure than normal, and saw her eyes widen in response. Surprise, however, was quickly doused by defiance.

Damien turned, letting her have the unhindered view of the happy couple, but unfortunately, the nature of the dance meant that every few bars he was faced with the sight of them again. And he couldn't help torturing himself by looking, by wondering *what if…*?

When he looked at his partner again she blinked slowly as a mischievous smile played on her lips. 'I'd thank you for the pleasure of dancing with you, but it would be a lie,' she said.

Damien knew he shouldn't rise to the bait, but his defences had been eroded by the acid of this happy day. 'Believe me,' he replied, 'the feeling is entirely mutual.'

Zoe smirked, and Damien's blood rose a few degrees in temperature. She wasn't supposed to be *enjoying* this. He wanted her off his back. Avoidance had failed. Charm had failed. The only artillery he had left in his current state of mind was the blunt truth.

'Look, I don't like you and you don't like me, but let's just get through this dance—for Luke and Sara's sake—then we can go our separate ways.'

And then, because looking at Zoe made him feel clammy and out of control, his gaze slid inevitably back to Sara.

Zoe twisted her head to follow his line of sight and then whispered in his ear, 'I've seen you watching them.'

That got his attention. That got his focus one hundred per cent back on his partner. An icy electric shock arced from his chest down to his stomach. She hadn't guessed, had she? Because, if Zoe knew his secret, there was no doubt in his mind that she would broadcast it far and wide.

'I'm happy for them,' he mumbled, and his feet

suddenly felt like bricks, causing him to miss a step.

Zoe's smirk grew, enveloping her in an aura of smugness. 'It's more than that,' she said and then her eyes widened a little—a penny dropping into place somewhere in the back of her head. 'There's something about what they've got, about *that*—' she pulled her hand from his and waved it in the direction of the bride and groom '—you can't keep your eyes off.'

Damien held his breath while Zoe began to laugh.

'Who'd have thought it? Damien *Stone*, not living up to his name, actually having an emotion other than pride for once.'

Pride? What was she talking about? He was a stand-up guy, someone to depend on in a crisis. What was proud about that? And how dare Zoe St James judge him?

'Well, at least I have some pride,' he countered. 'Having no sense of shame isn't considered an asset by most people.'

Her mouth dropped open and a little gasp slipped through her lips.

Damien couldn't hide his slow smile. Now he understood just why Zoe enjoyed firing off her little verbal darts so much. There was a lovely glow of satisfaction to be had when one hit home.

Her eyes narrowed. 'You stuck-up…unbearable…'

Now he was tempted to laugh, never having seen this woman without just the right sarcasm-laced word for any occasion. It was oddly gratifying to see her speechless, even for just a few seconds, because he was sure her talent wouldn't desert her for too long.

Unfortunately, his plan to silence her, to get her off his, backfired. It was then she decided to pull out the heavy artillery, get really personal.

'What is it about Luke and Sara that gives the great Damien Stone that faraway look in his eyes, I wonder? Just what is it that turns him into a big-eyed puppy dog with his tongue lolling out?'

Pins and needles tingled up Damien's spine. He knew she was spouting nonsense, just hunting for ammunition, but if she kept talking—and Zoe St James would *always* keep talking—she might just stumble onto the truth. He had to get her out of here. Out of earshot of any of the other wedding guests and especially Luke and Sara.

They weren't far from one of the entrances to the marquee now and, with a bit of nimble footwork, he spun her in that direction, then hauled her through the muslin-draped doorway. Once they were out into the cool night air, he dropped all pretence of dancing—dropped *her*—except for one hand, which he kept firmly clasped in his as he dragged her towards the formal gardens, ignoring her squeals of protest.

He marched down gravel paths edged with low box hedges towards the sound of running water. When they were far enough from the marquee not to be heard, or even to be stumbled upon, Damien put on the brakes and turned to face Zoe, throwing her hand back to her as if he'd been contaminated by its touch.

'What exactly is your problem?' he said, his voice thin from the effort of keeping a lid on his temper.

She held her hand to her torso with the other one, rubbing it furiously. 'Ow!' Her mouth stayed open as she searched for more words. When they came they were worth the wait.

'What's *my* problem?' She shook her head in disbelief. 'This, from the guy who is so far up his own backside he can probably see his tonsils!'

There it was. Zoe gold—although its properties

were closer to those of petrol as far as Damien was concerned.

'That's enough.' Far too much. She'd do well to heed the silky tone that had crept into his voice. When his employees heard it, they scarpered.

But Zoe, as always, didn't know when to stop, didn't know when too much was too much. She just battled on, pointing out his flaws, circling round the undiscovered truth, but getting closer to it every second.

He tried to shut her up by various methods: further warnings, ignoring her. He even tried to reason with her, but that runaway mouth just kept on jogging.

'I don't know what's got you all churned up today,' she said finally, her hands on her hips, her breath coming in short pants, which was emphasising the rise and fall of her breasts in a way Damien was trying very hard not to notice. 'Maybe you're just jealous because Luke has Sara and you've got no one. But until you can climb down off that self-made pedestal and act like a human being instead of something carved out of marble I doubt any woman would say yes to you anyway!'

Oh, Damien was feeling very human at this moment, thank you very much. Nothing cold and dead about his racing pulse, or the jumpy feeling that reminded him of a pressure cooker just about to pop its lid. He needed to move, to shout, to run, to do *something* to release whatever was building inside of him. And that sensation seemed to grow with every syllable spilling from Zoe St James's mouth.

She opened it again, and Damien decided he couldn't take another second. He had to shut that smart mouth up. And only one way came to mind.

It was stupid. Reckless. But the cocktail of stress, disappointment and adrenalin egged him on until he had no other option but to slip his hand behind Zoe's neck, drag her to him and kiss her.

Damien had marched her down a path that led to a large stone fountain with a wall surrounding it. Zoe grabbed onto it with one hand as the other made a mess of Damien's shirt, bunching it up so hard she doubted the creases would ever be erased. That flimsy grip on the cotton and his hand at the back of her neck were the only things that were preventing her from taking a swim.

Apart from his lips, of course.

She should pull away and slap him, shouldn't

she? Who the hell did he think he was? But she didn't pull away. She didn't slap him. Because, unfortunately, Mr Perfect was living up to his name in the kissing department too.

It started out hot and hard and…hot some more, but after a while it changed, slowed. The kiss became more about tasting and exploring than competing and raging. Zoe stopped gripping onto the fountain and placed that hand on his chest too, snaked it round his neck, matching him, as his long fingers uncurled and began to explore the fine hair that curled into ringlets at the base of her skull.

Damn her impulsive nature. It was entirely responsible for starting all of this. First of all, it had got hold of her mouth and had run away with it, then it had poked a stick at a caged tiger to see what it would do. And now it knew just what the tiger was capable of, it wasn't particularly inclined to stop!

This was Damien Stone, remember? Pull away.

He's not attracted to you. He doesn't even like you. And it shouldn't matter just how good he tastes or exactly what he's doing with his lips. Save yourself the humiliation and end this. And if you want to salvage some of that non-existent pride of yours, you need to end this first.

But Zoe had never been one for listening to advice. Especially her own.

And the kiss, although it was still slowing in tempo, was building in intensity. In fact, she thought the tops of her ears might have just caught fire. What was more, she really didn't care.

Damien had been kissing her for quite some time now, and he certainly seemed to be enjoying himself just as much as she was, seemed to be immersed in the moment. Of course she could be wrong. This could just be him on autopilot. But, crikey, if all this slow expertise was what he managed when he was only halfway invested, imagine what the full blast would be like! Forget the tips of her ears—she'd have to throw her entire body in the fountain.

She let go of his shirt, now creased beyond all hope, and explored his torso, running her fingers between jacket and shirt, letting her palms slide across his back.

Perhaps he did find her attractive after all. Maybe all that pent-up aggression and haughtiness had just been the Stone version of pigtail-pulling. She knew she shouldn't let it, but that thought burrowed deep inside her and started to glow. She couldn't stop it, not when she'd spent a lifetime being invisible to most men like him, men who were way out of her league. She sighed as Damien's lips left her mouth and headed towards her ear.

It was then they both heard footsteps on the gravel path. They both froze, not even coherent enough to pull hands and lips away from each other, ending up stuck together like a parody of Rodin's famous statue.

'Damien, there you are. Sara was looking for you a moment ago and, oh…um…sorry.'

It was Luke's voice. Zoe tried to shrink herself sideways. Not easy when you were as generously proportioned as she was. But at present Damien was shielding her from Luke's view, and for some reason he didn't want Luke to find out who he was with, and that was fine by her. She didn't want this moment of temporary insanity being reported round the wedding reception any more than he did.

But trust Damien to choose this moment to stop doing the perfect thing. He found the strength to move, stepped back and stared at her. The heat rushed from the top of her ears straight into her cheeks.

'Oh! *Zoe…!*' Luke was frowning and smiling at the same time, although the smile was starting to win. 'Sorry… Just didn't think you two… Like I said, I'll come back—' he grinned '—later.'

Footsteps on gravel again, getting quieter. And then it was just a trickle of the fountain, the rasp of their breath and the noise of the party from the marquee, otherworldly and muffled.

Neither of them spoke. Not with words. But Damien's face began to get very eloquent, and the emotions on display were not what a girl wanted to see after a kiss like that.

Shock. Confusion. Even a little bit of guilt, if she wasn't mistaken, although she couldn't guess why. His mouth pulled down and she felt as if he'd taken a huge step backwards, even though he hadn't actually moved. It was that last emotion that really put the cherry on top.

Disgust.

*That* was when she slapped him.

Damien was still rubbing his cheek as he ran back over the lawn towards the marquee. He wasn't sure if he'd deserved that slap or not. Surely, the time for hand to face contact would have been when he'd lurched towards her, not five minutes later when her arm had been hooked around his back, pulling her closer to him, and his teeth had been at her earlobe?

But, then again, maybe he should have saved her the bother and slapped himself first. What had he thought he was doing? Really? *Zoe St James?*

He shook his head, trying to put it down to some kind of mental breakdown, brought about by weeks of stress and then having to endure the worst day of his life, but his attempt at reasoning with himself kept getting side-tracked by thoughts of Zoe's supple lips, memories of how complete and unfettered her response had been. She certainly knew how to more than talk with that runaway mouth of hers, he thought wryly.

Okay, so he was attracted to her. They had chemistry. Weird things like that happened all the time. It was all down to pheromones and brain chemistry and strange evolutionary throwbacks.

But a girl like Zoe St James wasn't part of the picture he'd painted of his future, the one he'd been slowly piecing together like a jigsaw for the last decade. It didn't matter if they had enough chemistry together to power the New Year's fireworks in London—she just wasn't part of the plan. And Damien Stone always stuck to the plan.

'Luke!'

He caught his friend just as he was about to go back inside. Slightly breathless now, he pressed a hand to his chest. 'You said you wanted a word with me?'

Luke shook his head. 'I said *Sara* wanted a word with you.'

Sara.

A wave of guilt washed over Damien. He felt as if he'd been unfaithful, which was ridiculous.

Luke was grinning at him, waggling his eyebrows.

'Shut up,' Damien said.

Luke just grinned harder. 'Well, I can't say I wasn't surprised. I mean…Zoe… But it's good to see you being less of a hermit where women are concerned. You've been working too hard for far too long.'

Luke was wrong. It wasn't work that was the problem. Yes, Damien put in long hours occasionally, but Luke was under the impression that things were worse than they really were, because that was the excuse Damien trotted out when spending an evening with Sara and Luke at his house would be just too cosy to bear.

He pulled a face. Just when had he become this person? A person who skulked around hiding from everyone, lied to his friends and, yes, launched himself on unsuspecting women, even if the woman in question had deserved a bit of a comeuppance?

'So…' Luke clapped him on the back then gave him a one-armed hug '…are you going to see her again while we're away on honeymoon?'

Damien shook his head. He'd rather set himself on fire.

But there *was* something in what Luke had said. He'd spent too long pining for a woman who wasn't his, too long shutting himself off from all the other possibilities out there. Okay, Sara fitted perfectly in that ten-year plan of his—owning his business, buying a decent house, wife, kids—but that didn't mean no one else could ever fit that gap. He needed to readjust, and he could do it. He could.

It was time to move on.

What a pity he hadn't quite been able to let go of the *idea* of Sara before now. Maybe if he'd done it sooner, he would have been here with someone today and, instead of struggling on his own, feeling like a volcano that was trying to stop itself erupting. He might have enjoyed himself.

He tried to imagine what it would be like…

A faceless girl. Brunette—not blonde, like Sara—in a stylish dress. A woman who reached for his hand during the service, squeezed it as the vows were said.

But it didn't work. The fantasy morphed into a picture of him out by the fountain, taking Zoe by the hand, leading her back into the hotel, a slow, knowing smile on both their faces…

No.

Get a grip, Damien.

Luke's right. It's been too long. Those pent-up hormones are driving you screwy.

'*Relax*, mate!' His friend's hand was still on his shoulder and it began to knead the tense muscle there rather painfully. 'You know what you need?'

'A stiff gin and Angelina Jolie's phone number?'

Luke laughed. 'Nope. You need a holiday.'

Damien shook his head. The last thing he needed was endless days on his own, nothing to do, too much time to think. No, work was the answer. Work was always the answer.

And coming up with a new plan. A better one. An achievable one.

That thought stopped him in his tracks.

He'd fallen into the same trap as his father had, hadn't he? And he hadn't even realised it. If anyone should understand how much damage yearning for the impossible did, it was Damien Stone.

'So where's Sara, then? I thought you said she was looking for me?'

Luke nodded towards the inside of the marquee. 'Talking to her father at the table in the corner.' His smile became sappy. 'You can't miss her—just look for the most beautiful girl in the room.'

This morning a comment like that would have been a slap in the face, but Damien let it bounce off him. Time for a new plan, remember? And this time he wasn't going to let himself get derailed.

He would walk over to Sara and her father. He would listen to what she had to say, and then he would say goodbye.

To Sara. And the idea of Sara.

# CHAPTER FOUR

NOT many drivers were on the road at one in the morning to witness the sight of a bridesmaid shooting down the motorway in her car, foot to the floor, flowers in her hair. Zoe wouldn't have noticed them if they had. Her efficient little runabout didn't go much above seventy, but pressing the pedal all the way down gave her a small sense of satisfaction, something to counteract the growing sense of shame.

She'd never been so humiliated.

The look on his face…

As if he'd just committed some heinous crime. Even the thought of fit, blond Matthew as her own private deckhand for the next two weeks didn't cheer her up. Maybe she'd send him away and stay moored in the marina for the holiday, hiding out in the cabin and saving the other holidaymakers from her obviously disgusting presence.

But if there was one thing Zoe liked to do it was change her mind, and she did just that when she saw the bleary-eyed Matthew waiting for her in *Dream Weaver*'s cockpit.

Her wheel-along case had been making a terrible racket on the pontoons and must have woken him up. Along with the rest of the residents in the tiny marina halfway up the River Dart. She checked her watch—four-fifteen! Eek!—then tried to haul her case over the edge of the boat, but it was obvious her lightning-speed packing method—just throw everything she owned in—made that impossible. Matthew very gallantly hopped out of the boat and dealt with her luggage, giving her ample time to admire his fine physique.

'Sorry,' she said blithely, skipping on board and showing none of her guilt. 'I got here as fast as I could, but my car is a bit past it.'

Matthew shrugged and handed her the keys. He even smiled. 'No problem. Luke said he'd let me take *Dream Weaver* to France and back later in the summer if I helped you out. So for the next two weeks I'm all yours. Ready to fulfil your every whim.'

For the first time in six hours Zoe smiled. Now *that* was the kind of response a girl liked to hear.

Matthew looked her up and down and laughed

softly. 'Not sure about your sailing clothes, though.'

Zoe looked down, and then she laughed as well. 'Well, I suppose satin and trainers aren't the usual attire, but don't worry—' she patted her hundred litre case '—I've got more appropriate stuff in here.'

Matthew laughed even harder. 'I'll bet!'

He ran a hand through his delightfully tousled hair. 'Do you want to go out tomorrow? Maybe round to a beach?'

Zoe patted her suitcase again. 'Swimming cozzie is packed,' she said, and noticed a glitter of interest at that fact in the skipper's eyes. 'Why not?'

He checked his watch and frowned. 'What time do you want to get started?'

She waved a helpless hand. 'Oh…whenever. I like to go with the flow.'

Matthew nodded and grinned. Zoe grinned back. Kindred spirits. Oh, this holiday might just be what she needed after all. A summer fling, maybe, to restore her confidence in life, love and men in general.

However, thinking of men in general led to thinking of one man in particular. Her ears burned with shame while other places burned with something else entirely.

We're not thinking about him, she told herself. He's two hundred miles away, polishing his halo, probably, and the next two weeks is all about forgetting him and that…unfortunate…kiss ever existed.

Matthew handed over the key to *Dream Weaver*, a small square-ended piece of metal with a squash ball-sized piece of cork on a key ring, and then clambered off the boat and on to the pontoon.

'See you in the morning,' he said with a relaxed wave.

'Not *too* early, though,' Zoe added quickly.

Matthew nodded, one night owl to another. See? Kindred spirits.

Once she was alone again Zoe realised she was actually quite tired. She headed below decks. However, she'd forgotten that there weren't proper stairs leading down into the cabin, but what was more like two wooden boxes stacked on top of each other, with an extra little foot platform bolted onto the top one for those with shorter legs. She managed to manhandle the giant case down into the cabin without smashing it on the floor, then wrestled it past the seating area, past the tiny toilet she'd forgotten how to work, and into the two-man cabin at the front of the boat.

She plopped the case on one side of the V-shaped bunk and took a long hard look at the two narrow berths, separate at the head end, but joined together near the feet. Not a lot of room, and Zoe liked to sprawl. It was also a long way down to the hard wooden floor if she rolled out of bed during the night.

But then she remembered there was an extra section of wood that fitted between the two berths, making them one giant triangle, and a matching wedge of mattress to complete the jigsaw, and she went in search of it.

Once that was sorted, she rummaged through her case for her PJs, leaving her underwear and clothes where they fell, then squeezed herself into the tiny bathroom to get ready for bed. Thankfully, the instructions for the toilet were written on a plaque on the wall—but it still took her three attempts before she got it to work properly.

Within twenty minutes of getting on board, she was climbing into the soft cotton-lined sleeping bag that had been left out for her. Probably by

Matthew. She smiled as she closed her eyes and stretched her mouth wide in a silent yawn.

Oh, yes. This holiday was going to be just what she needed.

Dawn was just breaking as Damien hauled his soft sailing bag, compactly filled with everything he would need for the next week or two, down the steep jetty that led to the pontoons of Lower Hadwell's marina.

After weeks of being cooped up in a city office, or in the dust and noise of a construction site, it was blissful to feel the cold dawn breeze on his face, smell the salt and seaweed in the air. Even better would be the bacon sandwich he planned to make himself on board before setting off. Two weeks on board Luke's beloved boat, no one to please but himself.

It was the perfect plan. He'd be busy the whole time and he wouldn't have to talk to a soul if he didn't want to. And by the time he got back to his office in London he'd have made progress in wiping his best friend's wife from his mind—at least in any capacity other than 'family friend'.

He'd also do his best to forget that it had been

Sara's idea to use the boat now it was free. She'd square it with Luke in the morning, she'd said. But he knew his friend wouldn't mind. He'd taken *Dream Weaver* out many times before when he'd needed a bit of space and solitude.

The boat was quiet when he arrived but, strangely, unlocked. He found the key on the table in the middle of the seating area in the main cabin and threw his sailing bag down on one of the long benches that doubled as a berth. Probably that flaky Matthew who kept an eye on *Weaver* when Luke wasn't around. He'd have to have a word with him about that when he got back.

But for now…

Well, Damien was standing on a boat with the key in his hand and a whole river, then the Devon and Cornwall coast waiting to be explored. Why wait? He could sort out the bacon sandwich later. What he really wanted to taste right now was salt on his tongue. He couldn't wait for that moment of perfect silence when he got out to sea, winched up the sails and cut the engine.

Not wasting a second, he ran upstairs into the cockpit, turned the engine on and set about casting off.

\* \* \*

A distant rumble lulled Zoe as she dozed, and the gentle side-to-side movement of the boat rocked her back into a deep slumber. When she woke the sun was high in the sky, streaming through the glass hatch in the roof, and her face was squashed against the wall of the cabin. She was also pinned beneath her bright pink case.

Huh?

While she'd slept somebody had messed with the earth's gravity. Instead of everything heading straight down, the world was tilted at forty-five degrees. It was also very bumpy, and every few seconds her cabin would bounce off something and a hollow noise echoed round the boat's hull.

Was there a storm? The weather forecast had been good. Well, at least she'd imagined it was good because it had been bright and sunny for the last week, and Zoe wasn't the type to check that kind of thing religiously. If at all.

Large drops of water sprayed onto the hatch as the boat did its biggest lurch yet. Definitely a storm, then. But a strange kind of storm because, apart from those dull echoes from the underside of the boat, it was completely quiet. And why was the sun still shining?

She rubbed her eyes, got out of bed and braced

a hand against the wall to stop herself from falling over. Her brain struggled to make sense of the mismatched information being sent to it. She hadn't drunk much last night, so this couldn't be the hangover of all hangovers. What the heck was going on?

As she lurched her way through the cabin she glanced out of one of the tiny lozenge-shaped portholes and finally the jigsaw pieces began to come together. There was blue. Lots of it. Above and below the horizon. And cliffs. Last time she'd checked Lower Hadwell had been all about green hills covered in woods and sheep-filled fields. Not a cliff to be seen. Which left only one conclusion to stumble onto.

They were at sea. Almost. Right at the mouth of the estuary.

Matthew must be much more of a morning person than she gave him credit for. How disappointing. And she'd at least have expected him to discuss with her which beach she'd like to go to. Behaviour like this reminded her of someone she'd much rather push to the recesses of her mind and slap the label *What were you thinking?* on.

The breeze hit her full in the face and tugged at her hair as she emerged from the cabin. The cockpit was empty, and no one was at the large wooden tiller at the back end. She could hear the mainsail rustling frantically above her head as it flapped in the wind. She stepped out into the cockpit properly, stood on one of the non-slip benches and looked further down the boat.

There, clipping a sail onto the wire that ran from the front of the boat to the top of the mast, was a hunched figure. Zoe called and waved at Matthew, but the wind stole her words. She yelled louder.

And then she had another one of those *worst hangover ever* moments, because when the hunched man stood up and turned around his face was different and his hair was all wrong. In fact, it looked a lot like…

But it couldn't be!

Before she could tell her brain to start making sense, another large wave hit the boat—which she now realised had been responsible for the hollow bumping she'd heard in her cabin—and Zoe, who had not been on a yacht enough times before to know it was a good idea to hang onto something at all times, tumbled back into the cockpit.

Had that been the only thing that had happened, things would have been fine, apart from a few bruises and a general sense of embarrassment.

But Zoe fell against the tiller when she landed and grabbed onto it for support, causing the boat, which had been facing the wind, to swing round sharply. The mainsail filled and *Dream Weaver* pitched sideways.

Zoe righted herself just in time to see the shocked face of the man at the other end of the boat. Definitely not Matthew.

Definitely her worst nightmare.

Definitely losing his balance from the unexpected lurch of the deck. In slow motion, he grabbed for the wire he'd been clipping the sail onto but missed. For a couple of seconds he seemed to hover in mid-air, but then there was a splash and a yell, and Zoe's worst nightmare had fallen overboard.

Zoe freaked. For a moment she was frozen to the spot, her mouth opening and closing, her hands twitching as if they were grasping for something, as if their ineffectual motion could wind time backwards so she could catch him on the replay.

Then she screamed. Then she ran. Up the deck, hardly looking where she was going, until she reached the spot where he'd disappeared. Then she screamed a second time at the sight of Damien

Stone, half-consumed by the sea, clinging for dear life onto one of the metal posts that surrounded the deck.

There was no time for discussion of the surreal wormhole that had ruptured time and space to bring him here. Zoe just grabbed his wrist, anchored one foot against another one of the metal posts and pulled. For a while they seemed to make no progress. Between them, they managed to pull Damien up towards the deck, but another wave would hit *Dream Weaver*, causing him to slip back a couple of inches.

Eventually, Damien managed to pull himself up further and Zoe took handfuls of his clothes—anything she could get her hands on—and dragged and tugged and yanked until his chest and one foot were on the deck and he managed to haul himself back on board.

As soon as he hit the deck he jumped up and ran to the cockpit, where he grabbed a rope and loosened it. Zoe ran after him, and by the time she reached the cockpit the mainsail was down, hanging untidily in folds over the boom like a giant piping bag.

That was when Damien turned to face Zoe. That was also when the shouting began. Lots of words, lots of half sentences. Not a lot of sense. They both finally fell silent, regarding each other warily, ribcages heaving.

Damien's tone was low and dark. '*Please* tell me I'm hallucinating!'

Zoe's hands popped onto her hips. 'Charming! That's what I get for saving your life!'

'It was *you* who tipped me overboard!'

He wanted to cast accusations around? Fine. Zoe had plenty of her own.

'Well, if you hadn't practically kidnapped me… If you'd actually thought to inform me you were taking the boat out for a sail…' She paused and frowned. 'Hang on. What are you doing here anyway? Are you *stalking* me?'

Damien laughed so hard he almost fell overboard again. 'This really is an alternate reality, isn't it? And I should ask you what you're doing on board *Weaver*. You don't even know how to sail!'

She pulled herself up straighter. 'I *might* know how to sail. How would you know?'

Damien gave her one of his patented superior looks at that moment. It made her wish she'd let him flounder in the waves instead of breaking three nails fishing him out.

'Believe me, it's obvious,' he said dryly.

They stood there, at opposite ends of the cockpit, radiating irritation, neither of them willing to answer the other's question first, as if doing so would indicate surrender.

Damien blew air out through his mouth and shook his head, then he reached for the rope dangling into the cockpit, wound it round something that looked like an over-sized pepper grinder and started to hoist the sail. She sat down in the cockpit and folded her arms. 'Where are we going?'

Damien looked back over his shoulder as he secured the rope. He reached for the tiller, then sat down facing her. The boat started leaning again as the wind hit the triangle of white, and Zoe was childishly pleased that she was on the upper side. At least she was until Damien turned the boat around so it pitched again, and then he was smiling down at her, his lips thin, and she was glowering back at him, her arms folded so tight now they felt like a corset.

'I'm taking you back to the marina,' he said finally.

Zoe frowned harder. 'Why me?'

Damien looked at her as if she should have been in a straitjacket. 'So you can collect your stuff and disembark. I don't know what kind of stupid joke you are trying to pull—'

'Listen, Mr—' Zoe stood up, but forgot to factor in the wonky floor and sat straight back down again. 'Luke told me I could use his boat for the next couple of weeks, so I'm not going anywhere.'

That wiped the smug smile off his face. 'But Sara told me...'

They looked at each other.

'Double booked,' they both said in unison.

Then they sat in silence, trying to cogitate what that might mean.

'You don't think they *meant* to...' Zoe said, shaking her head.

Damien was doing the same. 'No. They wouldn't. They know I don't like—'

Zoe raised her eyebrows and the rest of the sentence stayed unsaid.

'It must be some kind of mistake,' he added, having the decency to look at least a little sheepish.

Zoe looked out to sea, as if searching for answers there. 'We could always call them and ask them if...' Zoe trailed off and her gaze returned to Damien, who looked every inch the competent sailor as he nudged the tiller this way and that, every now and then checking the compass or looking out to a spot on the headland.

He lifted one side of his mouth in a wry smile.

'You're right,' she said. 'Not a good time to be phoning the happy couple, first day of their honeymoon and all.'

Damien's mouth thinned into a straight line again and he looked away.

'We're just going to have to work this one out on our own, then.'

Zoe nodded, and then she shivered. She'd been so taken up in rescuing Damien, then wanting to rip his head off, that she'd totally forgotten she was only wearing her pyjamas—a soft grey vest and a pair of pink and grey striped bottoms.

Damien must have caught her shudder out of the corner of his eye, because he turned his head and looked at her again.

'Why don't you go below deck and get warm?'

If Zoe had been a cat, the fur along her spine would have just risen straight up. She opened her mouth.

'Oh, calm down,' he said dismissively, and when she looked as if she was about to do the opposite he made an observation. 'You're a little bit wet,' he added.

'So are you,' she countered.

'Yes,' said Damien, looking her up and down, 'but I'm dressed for sailing and I don't think that fabric you have on is very…water repellent.'

Zoe was about to argue, but then she glanced down and saw what he meant. Her vest was plastered to her, soaked front and back, and her trousers weren't much better. She glared at him. He couldn't have mentioned this sooner? Or he couldn't have taken a hot poker and burnt out his eyes?

She got up with as much dignity as she could muster, and then wobbled her way across the cockpit and down the stairs, mightily glad that after the first few steps he couldn't see her front any more, couldn't see the vest moulded to her rather impressive chest.

She didn't, however, realise that the striped fabric clung just as lovingly to her bottom. And she didn't see Damien lean over a little bit to watch her ample rear end wiggle its way into her cabin and disappear.

# CHAPTER FIVE

AN UNEASY truce was established over bacon sandwiches a short while later. Damien took the boat to a little cove just near the estuary and dropped anchor. And Zoe, who was now warm and dry and dressed, fried the bacon while Damien took a quick shower and got himself into the same state.

The truce held, of course, because neither of them said much to each other. However, that couldn't continue indefinitely, so once butties had been eaten and washed down with tea, it was time to retreat to their corners and fight this thing out.

Damien had decided as he drove down that morning that sailing was just about the only thing he could think of that would keep him sane over the next couple of weeks, that sailing and sailing alone would dislodge the unwanted fantasies in his head. He really didn't want to hand *Dream Weaver* over to this woman—a woman who probably wouldn't even untie her from her mooring. It was almost criminal to leave the boat neglected like that.

But underneath that sense of indignation he also had the horrible creeping feeling that he would end up doing the chivalrous thing, even though he'd rather be eaten by sharks first. The knowledge only served to make him more irritable. He drained the last of his tea, plonked his mug down on the propped-up wing of the table and looked at Zoe.

'What were your plans?' he asked in a perfect impression of calm and reasonableness.

Zoe tucked a strand of wet hair behind her left ear. She seemed slightly unnerved by his politeness, and Damien had a flashback to the night before, when she'd kissed him without reserve or barrier, and he'd sensed a hint of vulnerability beneath that brassy armour.

But they weren't here to think about kissing— they were here to talk about sailing, remember?

She swallowed. 'Just…you know. Having a break—a holiday.'

Damien frowned. 'You weren't going to take *Weaver* out on your own, were you?'

A spike of irritation totally eradicated any hint

of vulnerability in Zoe's eyes. That was better. He preferred that.

'No,' she replied, the space between her eyebrows puckering, 'I'm not that stupid, whatever you might think!'

Damien took a deep breath. He was going to stay in control. He was.

'I was going to explore Lower Hadwell and maybe Dartmouth, read, sunbathe—and Luke had arranged a skipper for me for a few days so we could go out sailing.'

Damien nodded. He knew he should do the decent thing, but the bobbing of the boat beneath him on the swell, the familiar slap of the steel shrouds against the mast, teased him. He really didn't want to get back in his car and drive all the way back to London. It had been too long since he'd had the opportunity to sail like this. Maybe Luke had been right. Maybe he *had* been working too hard.

She folded her arms across her chest, and he knew she was digging in for a fight, that he might not get her off this boat unless he tied her up, popped her in a sail bag and drove her all the way back home in the boot of his car. He allowed himself a little daydream to that effect before he made himself face reality, and a stony-faced Zoe, again.

Just looking at her made him restless and jumpy—and in two completely different ways. How did she do that? How did his body respond to those curves when his mind was yelling *No way*?

And then an idea occurred to him. Both beautiful and idiotic at the same time.

At least while Zoe had been needling him at the wedding he'd forgotten about Sara. She might drive him crazy, but she was one hell of an effective distraction. And, much as he might wish it so, she wasn't going anywhere. He knew she'd never cave and let him have the boat for the fortnight. For some reason she took everything he said or did very personally. So maybe he could make all her irritating qualities work for him rather than against him.

'Why don't I be your skipper?'

Zoe stopped moving. Her chest didn't rise and fall, her eyelids didn't blink. 'What?' she said so quietly he almost didn't hear her.

'You want two weeks relaxing in the sun—or whatever weather we get. This is England, after all—and I want to sail…'

She nodded, very softly, very slowly.

'I know we…clashed…yesterday—' He'd almost said *kissed*, but that hadn't been his intention at all. He cleared his throat and continued. 'But it was a stressful day for everyone, emotions were running high…'

His voice dried then. He went to take a sip of tea, but discovered too late his mug was already empty, and had to make do with swallowing once or twice.

Zoe leaned forward slightly, and her eyes lost that narrow, suspicious look. 'You'd be my personal deck hand?'

That wasn't quite the way he'd have put it, but he wasn't going to quibble about it. This way, they could both get what they wanted.

'I suggest we both use the boat. I can sail. You can sunbathe or shop or do whatever you want to do, and we can stay out of each other's way. Same boat, separate holidays.' It sounded so reasonable he almost believed it himself.

Zoe blinked, and Damien decided that without that hard, garish persona of hers in place—the one that made her headbutt life like a nanny goat— she was actually quite pretty.

Unfortunately, Zoe didn't stay quiet and almost ladylike for long. He saw the moment the insolence crystallised around her like a shell. She folded her arms across her front and rested back against the padded bench that would probably double as his bed that night.

'You're on,' she said with a twinkle in her eye, and Damien had to fight the urge to smile. 'To separate holidays.' She lifted her mug and toasted him with the remainder of her tea. 'And a truce. I can do it if you can.'

Ah, they were back to that—competition. Oh, well. It was something he and Zoe knew how to do excessively well, and as long as they were both trying to outdo each other being polite and accommodating, things should go pretty well.

Zoe sat in the cockpit, her feet up on the opposite bench, with a book in her lap and a large baggy shirt on over her swimming costume. It was still a bit chilly this morning to start sunbathing, which actually suited her fine at present. She was going to have to work up to baring substantial amounts of flesh now she had an audience. Once again she wished she had her best friend's figure. Sara had slender thighs, a flat stomach and an uncanny ability to say no to cake. Zoe, not so much—as her jelly-like thighs, bulging one-piece and general lumpiness bore witness to.

If only Mr Damien Stone weren't so…well…good-looking. She'd feel more comfortable stripping off if her companion had a white, pasty pigeon chest and legs like two knotted pieces of string. No such luck. Even under his jeans and T-shirt, it was obvious his body was every bit as perfect as the rest of him.

*A fact you know only too well, Zoe St James, since you were freely exploring it with your fingertips not even twenty-four hours ago.*

That was then, she told herself. This is now. And she wasn't going to mention that kiss, not if Damien wasn't. She wasn't going to weaken first. Bringing it up would only make it seem that she was some kind of desperate girly who had fallen under his spell. No way was she letting him think he had the upper hand.

Unwittingly, Damien Stone had engineered his own downfall. His suggestion had played right into her hands, because she was going to make him pay for that look on his face after he'd kissed her. He'd practically agreed to be her personal slave, and she was going to make the most of it.

By the end of this holiday he'd know she could do *disdain* just as well as he could.

In fact, the whole situation might be deeply satisfying on so many levels. Teaching him a lesson would be cathartic, because it really wasn't about him alone. It was all men like him, who thought everyone was beneath them, who needed to be taught a lesson. Men like her ex. Well, she was going to make sure Damien Stone felt way, way beneath her this holiday. A little humiliation might just be on the menu.

They'd sailed back into the Dart estuary and up to Lower Hadwell marina. Ever since they'd tied the boat up—Zoe knew there was a proper name for that, but it escaped her—Damien had been running around the boat like a mad thing. He'd opened all sorts of hidden lockers that she'd had no idea existed, checking sails and ropes and things she couldn't identify.

He'd pulled charts from the small desk that was opposite the tiny galley by the stairs that led to the cockpit, and then had spent ages muttering to himself and poring over them, and now he was up the other end of the boat doing heaven knew what. You'd have thought they were planning a transatlantic crossing, not two weeks puttering up and down the River Dart. At least, she'd assumed that was the plan. That had been *her* plan, anyway.

'Hey, deck hand!' she called, without looking up.

Damien's head appeared through the hatch right beside her, and her book jumped out of her lap. She scrambled to pick it up. How on earth had he got down there? Last time she'd seen him he'd been up the pointy end of the boat.

'Yes.'

Zoe took a moment to reply. He'd been so absorbed in whatever he'd been doing that he'd forgotten to put on that habitual frown he always seemed to wear when he looked at her. And without the suit—Damien always seemed to be wearing a suit—he looked younger and less stuffy. In fact, that look on his face was the distracted one her brothers had used to wear when they'd got into one of their aircraft modelling frenzies, the sort that meant they looked stressed but were actually enjoying every second.

'We're not planning on heading for Newfoundland or anything, are we?'

Now the frown was back. That hadn't taken long.

'No…' he said, sounding as if he was expecting it to be a trick question.

She gave one shoulder a breezy shrug. 'Just wanted to know, that's all.'

He turned to back down into the cabin. Zoe waited until he was a couple of steps down and then said, in her sweetest, most feminine voice, 'And, oh…Damien?'

A second of silence and then she heard his foot heavy on the step and his head appeared again.

'I'm thirsty,' she said, tipping her head on one side and squinting at him. 'Could you bring me a drink?'

Damien found that funny. At least, that was what she guessed the slight quirk of one eyebrow was all about.

'What?' she said, putting her book down and sitting up straighter. 'You're supposed to be my deck hand for the next two weeks—that was the deal, wasn't it?'

'Oh, that's the deal,' Damien said, still smiling. 'But I didn't agree to be your galley slave and personal servant. You need to get your terms right before you enter into contracts you don't understand.'

Zoe's mouth dropped open.

'So,' Damien said as he turned and headed back into the cabin, 'you can get your own drink. I'm going back to doing what a good deck hand should do—getting this boat ready to sail. I reckon we can get as far as the Isles of Scilly if we get going this afternoon.'

That had Zoe on her feet and following him into the cabin. 'The Isles of Scilly?' she squeaked. 'What are you talking about?'

Damien turned round from where he was flicking switches above the map desk on something that Zoe guessed might be a radio. 'You wanted me to sail the boat for you, so I'm going to sail it. That was my part of the deal. We can get all the way down the Devon and Cornwall coast if the weather's good, stopping at different towns and villages every night.' He pointed at a chart laid out on the desk. 'Once we've rounded Lizard Point we can head for Land's End and after that the Scillies.'

'But—'

Zoe was about to argue, but an image popped into her head: wide, flat rippled sand at low tide, fringed by rock pools covered in glistening emerald seaweed. Bantham Beach.

Her aunt had had a coffee table book of Britain's best beaches when Zoe had been small. When they visited the rest of the family would come to blows over a game of Monopoly, but Zoe would curl up in an armchair with that book and imagine what it would be like to visit all those different beaches, and some of her favourites had been in this part of the world.

Now she had a chance to see them for herself—and not by trudging through sand dunes or hiking down cliff paths, laden like a packhorse with coolbags and blankets and windbreakers. No, she'd get to sail right up to them, be one of those elusive and glamorous people she'd sometimes seen from the sand, the ones on the glossy white boats who *had* to be somebody important. Okay, Luke's old boat wasn't exactly glossy and expensive, but it would do. And she'd always wanted to have an excuse to say, *Just popping back to the yacht, dahling...*

'Are you up for it?' Damien asked, startling Zoe out of her fantasy.

Zoe chewed her lip. This way, with Damien to do all the donkey work, all she had to do was lie back and enjoy it. 'Cruising round the Devon and

Cornwall coast?' she said, and surprised herself by smiling. 'Yes. I think I am.'

This is the life, Zoe thought, as she lay stretched out on the deck, just in front of the mast. The sun was warm on her skin, but the pleasant breeze filling the sails stopped those rays from scorching, and the gentle slap of the waves against the hull was lulling her into a half-doze.

Damien was off somewhere keeping himself busy, which was just how she liked it. He'd told her with grave seriousness that they were going to be heading across Start Bay, round the point and into Salcombe and there they would stop for the night. Zoe didn't care particularly where they went or where they stopped as long as the sun kept shining and she'd have a glass of wine in her hand when the sun went down. Until then Damien Stone could keep out of her way.

She'd much rather pretend he was some faceless minion, there to do her bidding. And, while she doubted very much he'd play along, at least while she was off doing her thing and he was off doing his, she could keep the fantasy alive. He might be useful to her at present, but that didn't mean she hadn't forgotten that kiss—or, to be more precise, the look *after* the kiss—and she intended to make him pay at some point. Until then she was lulling him into a sense of false security, playing nice.

Zoe's lids were already closed and the world behind them was pale pink and blurry, lit up by the afternoon sun, but it wasn't long before she wasn't aware of sunshine or waves any more and she fell into a deep and lazy sleep.

She woke when a chilly breeze danced across her bare shoulders. While she'd slept she'd rolled over onto her front, and now she peeled her face off her forearm and peered fuzzily towards the back of the boat.

A dark shape was there by the tiller. Damien. The brightness seemed to have gone out of the sky. She turned her head to get her bearings and realised they had left the long pebble-beached bay behind them and had now turned round the headland and were heading into the Salcombe Kingsbridge estuary. It was windier here and the sun was much lower in the sky, skulking behind low grey clouds and blessing them with bright haloes.

She sighed. If the rest of the holiday went like this it would be perfect.

It was time to move, though, before she fused

with the deck and became a strange kind of beached figurehead, stuck to the top of the boat instead of the front. She pushed herself up on one arm. That was when the pain began.

'Ow...!' Her back was tight and burning fiercely. 'Ow, ow, ow!'

She collapsed down onto the deck again and tried another approach, rolling over onto her side and then pushing herself up. More pain. None of it suffered in silence.

Zoe didn't have to look in the mirror to know what had happened. She was sunburned. Always a risk with her colouring, but she'd applied a high factor sun cream all over before lying down. Just how long had she been asleep up here?

Gingerly, she made her way along the boat and down to the cockpit, dreading the smirk she just *knew* would be plastered all over her sailing companion's face. She straightened up and ignored the stinging of her back and arms, not wanting to give him the satisfaction of seeing just how pathetic she was.

But when she stepped down into the cockpit, she was in for a surprise. Damien had been staring somewhere far ahead of the boat, lost in his own thoughts, but he glanced over when he heard the thud of her foot hitting the cockpit bench and his neutral expression quickly changed to a look of horror.

Zoe held a hand up to her face, which she was now aware was stinging just as badly as her back. And then she jumped down the steep stairs into the cabin, ignoring the pain it caused, and rushed for the little bathroom and checked out the damage in the mirror above the sink.

When she first saw her reflection she wanted to cry. Her face smarted. Well, to be more accurate, *half* her face smarted. The right half, which had been turned towards the sun while she'd slept, was a bright angry red. The left side was its usual pasty self, marred only by the vestiges of pale childhood freckles.

She looked like a freakish Halloween mask! How on earth was she going to go out in public looking like this? People would point and stare— and snigger, probably. She'd be banished to the cabin for at least a few days until it calmed down. Hardly the perfect holiday! And wouldn't Damien be pleased? With her locked away in her cabin he could pretend she wasn't there.

There was a soft knock at the bathroom door and Zoe jumped and banged her elbow on the wall—it was little more than a cupboard with a toilet, a sink and shower head above the couple of square feet of standing space.

'Are you okay?' Damien said, sounding far too genuine for Zoe's liking.

'I'm fine,' she snapped back, and she discovered her eyes had now added themselves to the inventory of body parts that stung.

Don't let him be nice to me, she prayed silently, holding her breath in an attempt to halt the moisture threatening to breach her bottom lashes. I don't want to think of Damien Stone as being nice.

Because that would mean she'd have to like him. And if she didn't despise him, she'd have no defences against that slow-humming attraction she'd been trying to fend off since a couple of stupid rumba steps had blindsided her.

Okay, most people would say that being attracted to a good-looking man wasn't a crime, but Zoe knew better. She knew how utterly seductive attention from a man who was way out of a girl's league could be. For a moment it made her feel special, made her believe she was worth something. But she also knew how those things ended, and she was well aware of her own propensity for falling hard and fast, ignoring all her own warnings to hold back, stay safe. So she wasn't looking Damien in the eye again, no matter how nice he was being, until she had her defences back in place.

So, a few minutes later, rather than heading back into the main seating area and galley, she slunk off into her own cabin and shut the door tightly behind her. She didn't come out again until the boat was stationary and she could hear the bustle of a busy marina all around.

Damien was sitting at the map desk with a large tube of aftersun in front of him. Trust Mr Perfect to have packed the essentials. He threw it to her and she caught it one-handed, and couldn't help feeling slightly cheered at the flicker of respect she saw in his eyes.

'Thanks,' she said, and sloped back off to her cabin to put it on. Her swimsuit was cut low at the back, though, and although she contorted herself into various positions to try and reach every bit of throbbing skin, there was a patch in the middle, just below her shoulder blades, that she couldn't quite reach.

Once she'd soothed the angry skin, she eased herself out of her costume. This took at least a couple of minutes, as she avoided dragging it across her skin or letting the elasticated straps slap back anywhere too tender. And then she put on a long, brightly coloured strapless sundress with a wide elasticated section round the bust. The ruched top pinched the area she hadn't been able to reach with the aftersun, but it was worth it to not have to deal with straps of any sort.

Then she set to trying to disguise her harlequin face with half a bottle of foundation. She ended up looking like her ballroom dancing teacher did just before a competition, but at least it was an even orangeness instead of half white, half pink.

That accomplished, she ventured out into the cabin and started hunting through the small cupboards surrounding the galley. At times like these, a girl needed something sweet.

She heard Damien thud down the steps from the cockpit. 'Looking for something?'

She nodded and kept ferreting through the cupboards, although she didn't know why—there was hardly anything in them. Damien had gone shopping at the tiny general store before they'd left Lower Hadwell, but all Zoe could find was some bread, some cheese, a few tins of beans, tea bags, coffee, long-life milk…

She twisted her head to look at Damien and winced; it felt as if she were giving herself a Chinese burn. 'Where are the biscuits?'

Damien's eyebrows rose a millimetre. 'What biscuits?'

Zoe blinked in disbelief. No biscuits?

'What about the chocolate?' she asked, her voice wavering slightly.

Damien just shook his head.

Zoe untwisted her poor neck, stood up and turned to face him. He was lounging in the hatchway, one foot on a higher step, one arm resting on the roof of the galley.

'Some deck hand you are! I thought you said you went shopping.'

Damien's mouth curled at one side. 'I did. But I did tell you it was just a quick shop to get the essentials, and that we'd stock up at the supermarket here tomorrow morning.'

'Chocolate *is* essentials!' Zoe cried, her plummeting sugar levels making her sound just a little desperate.

'Like I said, we can get other supplies in the morning. A whole case of chocolate, if you want.'

Now he was mocking her. And Zoe didn't like being mocked.

'Just a little bit for emergencies is enough, thank you very much,' she mumbled.

Damien just shrugged. He didn't say anything else. Didn't pick a fight—which left them both standing there, him towering above her half in, half out of the hatch, and Zoe suddenly realised how close they were. And then she realised how difficult it was to be anything *but* this close on a boat this size.

Damn it, if her non-pink cheek didn't flame to life to match the other one at that point. Thank goodness for the relative gloom of the galley and a layer of foundation her plasterer brother would have been proud of.

Damien held out his hand, and Zoe eyed it suspiciously.

'If you're really in need of nutrition, why don't we go and grab some dinner?'

Zoe obviously let her feelings regarding that suggestion show on her face because Damien gave her a weary look.

'Surely we can be adult enough to eat at the same table without starting World War Three. I'm starving, and there are plenty of restaurants nearby. I just can't be bothered to argue about it tonight.'

While Zoe didn't really want to spend any more time with Damien than was necessary, she was feeling more than a little sorry for herself, and the idea of letting someone else do all the thinking, all the planning, was rather appealing. She was all for delegating whenever she got the chance and, since her business meant she was a one-woman operation she really didn't get an opportunity to delegate that much, and she supposed Damien's proposal was reasonable enough.

But she ignored Damien's hand, retreating further back into the cabin. 'I'm just going to…er… go and get a wrap for my shoulders,' she muttered.

No hand-holding with Damien Stone, okay?

Last time she'd taken his hand willingly was when they'd swapped partners on the dance floor, and look how well *that* had turned out.

*But he can't find you too disgusting if he's willing to touch you again, even if he's just being polite.*

Yes, but he might change his mind again, like he did last time, and she couldn't have that. Better to keep as much of a distance as possible, especially as whenever she got within five feet of him she couldn't help remembering how strong and sure his arms had felt around her or just how expert those lips were. So she made sure she trailed behind Damien as they got off the boat and negotiated the metal wires that ran round the deck without assistance, even though the long skirt of her dress threatened to wrap itself round them.

No, who would want to put themselves in line for humiliation twice in twenty-four hours? Definitely not her.

# CHAPTER SIX

ZOE got her wish. By the time the sun was setting she was sitting on a restaurant terrace, high up on a hill above the estuary with a glass of perfectly chilled white wine in her hand. Bliss. Delicious seafood smells wafted from inside the trendy but reasonably priced restaurant and her stomach gurgled in anticipation. The breeze was soft, still clinging to the memory of the sunshine that had filtered through it all day, and the sky was a frosty blue, warming to primrose at the horizon.

Even Damien was behaving himself. He'd let her choose the restaurant, and he hadn't got all caveman-like when she'd insisted on paying her share.

Their starters arrived. Zoe had chosen a crab-meat timbale, covered in smoked salmon, but when she saw Damien's deep-fried lime and chilli king prawns she couldn't help thinking that she'd chosen hastily, and that maybe she should have perused the whole menu instead of just plumping for the thing that jumped out at her first. She couldn't help counting down the prawns as Damien worked his way mechanically through them.

Eventually, when there were only two left, Damien shook his head, glanced heavenwards and held one out to her by its tail. 'I can't eat with you staring at me like that. You might as well have one.'

*I couldn't possibly.*

That *should* have been the response that sprang instantly to her lips, but she was so transfixed by the bubbly golden batter and the sweet hot chilli sauce that glistened and threatened to sully the clean white tablecloth that she completely forgot to utter it. Saliva pooled in the bottom of her mouth.

Part of her didn't want to take anything from this man, but that part was quickly clubbed over the head and locked in a cupboard by the part of her that was licking its lips.

Moving quickly—so as not to hijack herself by coming over all appropriate—she leaned forwards, opened her mouth and closed her lips round the prawn, biting it off near the tail. She couldn't quite help closing her eyes as she savoured the sweetness and acidity of the dipping sauce, then the crunchy texture of the batter, and finally the firm flesh of the prawn beneath. A perfect pairing of opposites in so many ways. She let a little murmur of satisfaction out before opening her eyes again.

When she did, she found Damien in exactly the same position he'd been when she'd closed them, hand still outstretched, the remains of the prawn tail still pinched between finger and thumb. And he had a rather strange expression on his face. What was up with him?

He seemed to realise what he was doing, because suddenly he pulled his arm back and dropped the tail on his plate. Then he stared at the one remaining curl of battered seafood before dunking it in the sauce and holding it up in front of him, looking at it as if he'd never seen one before in his life.

Was this some weird kind of delayed seasickness that had got him in its grip? Zoe didn't know. But anything that took his critical focus off her and onto something else must be a good thing.

Up until now he'd been eating the prawns and accompanying salad as if it was a task to be got through, something to be ticked off an invisible list inside his head, no satisfaction to be had until the job was done, but now he closed his eyes and chewed slowly.

She could see it in his face—the revelations brought by each new taste and texture. She could almost feel her own taste buds responding as the different flavours hit his tongue. And then it was Zoe's turn to find herself frozen in position. A warm, fizzing lightning bolt shot through her, starting at the top of her head and raising goose-flesh as it travelled down her body to her toes. She shook herself slightly to quell the feeling of bubbles dancing along her skin. She quickly picked up a fork and attacked her forgotten crabmeat just as Damien opened his eyes again.

It's nothing, she told herself. Just a residual tingle from the kiss last night. It doesn't mean you fancy Damien Stone.

She scooped the rest of her crab up and stuffed it into her mouth in one go. The cool creamy taste would eradicate the memory of that prawn, get her back to normal again. She hoped.

And more conversation would be good. Something to distract her from the ideas of eating and tasting. And, from the looks of him, Damien needed distraction too. He was staring at his empty plate as if it held all the answers of the universe.

Pick a topic, Zoe. Any topic. It's not normally a problem for you, is it?

'So, how did you meet Luke?' she blurted out, her mouth only just emptied of crab. 'I know you've been friends for years, but I don't really know how it all began.'

Probably because she made a habit of tuning out or finding someone else to talk to whenever Damien had been around before.

She had, hadn't she?

It hadn't been a conscious thing, at least not at first. But he reminded her of that love-rat Aiden, so she'd steered clear, but after a while Damien had earned the dubious honour of irritating her completely on his own merits.

He had that same kind of I-rule-the-world confidence that Aiden had. However, when—like Damien—you headed a construction company that had just won a contract to erect buildings that would change the London skyline, you were probably entitled to be a little pleased with yourself.

But it bothered Zoe. Mostly because she had personal knowledge of just what was under that layer of confidence in a man like that. Nowhere near as pretty as the packaging, that was certain.

And she should know—she'd been engaged to it once.

How could one prawn result in such a profound experience?

Damien liked good food, would have said he enjoyed it, but in the end it was just calories and fats and proteins. Fuel, basically, no matter how much you dressed it up. But then he'd watched Zoe eat that prawn, her eyes sliding closed in obvious pleasure, and he'd realised he'd eaten six of the things already and had got none of that level of satisfaction. So he'd decided to try it her way.

And...wow.

Stopping for a moment, taking time to savour the tastes and textures, had been a totally new experience, and he wasn't sure what to do about it. He decided to put it on the backburner and let it simmer for a while. He also needed to find something to do to stop him thinking over and over again about Zoe's lips closing around that prawn.

'You wanted to know how I met Luke?'

Zoe sipped her wine and nodded.

'Both of our families used to rent holiday cottages down here—the same ones each year—at least until…' He stopped himself. She didn't need to know that. It was too personal. 'Until I was about fifteen. Luke and I were roughly the same age, so we teamed up occasionally, but it was the year we both begged our parents to enrol us in sailing school that the friendship really began. We bonded over a shared love: wind, waves, water— and finding the fastest way to travel across them.'

'So why don't you have a boat? I presume you don't, otherwise you wouldn't be borrowing Luke's.'

That was a good question. A very good question, actually. Zoe was as sharp as she was blunt. Interesting.

'I plan to,' he said. It had always been part of the plan: establish the business, settle down, buy a house, then maybe he'd think about a boat. 'It's just not been the right time yet.'

Zoe pulled her mouth downwards. 'That's a pity. You seem to love it so much. Why wait?'

Because…

Because he didn't like doing things out of order, or changing a perfectly good plan for no other reason than it might be fun. Succumbing to those self-indulgent urges was what had caused his father to destroy their family. As a result, Damien was rather suspicious of things with a feel-good factor. He weighed decisions to engage in such activities carefully. But he couldn't say something like that to someone like Zoe. She'd never understand.

'I just haven't found the perfect boat yet,' he replied finally. That sounded better.

Zoe pulled her napkin off her lap and placed it back on the table before leaning back in her chair and twisting her head slightly to take in the view.

Take in the view… That was the right phrase to describe what she did. She didn't just look at the fork of the estuary, the little sailing boats left impotent on a mud bank now the tide had receded, or the white dots of the seagulls circling above them. She seemed to engage in it, draw it all into herself using every sense at her disposal.

She turned and looked at him. 'So why not buy a "good enough for now" boat and enjoy that until the perfect one comes along?'

Hmm. He hadn't thought of that. And he didn't like admitting a different plan would be better than the one he'd already set in stone.

'I don't have to,' he said rather smugly. 'I can borrow Luke's.'

Zoe smiled reluctantly. 'It's nice that you share things. He's like a brother to you, isn't he?'

Damien nodded. Being an only child, he didn't know much about that sort of thing, but he'd imagined that was what having a brother might have been like. Thoughts of his friendship with Luke inevitably led to comparisons with Zoe and Sara's relationship. No one would ever describe those two as sisters. Opposite ends of the spectrum, maybe, but never sisters. He decided to satisfy his curiosity on that front.

'What about you and Sara? You must go back a long way as well.'

Zoe's face blossomed into the most beautiful smile at the mention of her friend's name, and Damien couldn't help letting his lips curl up a little too as they shared that particular mental picture.

'We've known each other since school. Sara was one of the popular girls…' She frowned and looked intently at him. 'Not the *mean* variety. I just meant that everyone wanted to be like her.'

'Did you?' He hadn't meant to let that question pop out, but out it had come. Too late to call it back now.

For a moment Zoe looked as if she was going

to say something biting and sarcastic, but her expression suddenly softened. 'Maybe. I was in awe of her a bit, I suppose. I didn't really understand why she befriended me.' She gave Damien a sardonic look. 'I don't know if you've noticed this, but I seem to be very talented at rubbing people up the wrong way.'

'No kidding.' But he smiled as he said it, and the glitter of challenge that ignited in Zoe's eyes softened instantly into humour.

He had the oddest sense that there was more to Zoe St James's outrageous remarks than just having no filter between brain and mouth. She chose to be that way, he realised. Chose to act that way, even though she'd just come out straight and told him she knew the effect it had on others. Why would anyone do that?

Their main courses arrived and Damien jokingly pushed his plate in Zoe's direction, one eyebrow raised. She rolled her eyes and shook her head.

'I think I'll stick with my tuna, thanks.'

Damien picked up his knife and fork and began carving his steak precisely. 'You say that now, but I don't want you staring lovingly at my plate for the next half-hour. It would drive me crazy—a bit like having someone read over your shoulder.'

Zoe shrugged as she chewed her first bit of tuna. 'I never did understand why that was such a problem. I read over people's shoulders all the time.'

Damien shook his head and reached for the salt. 'Anyway…So you kept in touch with Sara after school?' He felt slightly guilty even saying her name, but it seemed their mutual admiration for Sara was the one thing he and Zoe had in common, and the lull in their sparring was actually quite pleasant.

She nodded and swallowed her mouthful. 'I suppose lots of people lose touch with friends after school, but Sara's very loyal.' She looked down at her plate and lines appeared on her forehead.

'What?'

Her bottom lip protruded slightly and she looked thoughtful.

'Odd, isn't it?' she said, looking back at him. 'The things you remember from your school days. Kids can be so cruel…'

Damien leaned forward. 'What did they say?'

Zoe gave him a lopsided smile. 'You think, with this hair and this figure they didn't have plenty of ammunition? Can't you guess?'

Damien could imagine it. Even worse, he felt ashamed he'd thought the same thing himself. Kids would pick on anything that marked someone out as different. But Zoe's hair wasn't ugly because it was different. Look at it now—the edges of those unruly curls lit up gold by the setting sun.

She flicked those very same curls back off her face and looked at him, her chin raised a notch. 'They didn't say anything I hadn't heard before. I've got four older brothers. Believe me, I can dish it out just as good as I can take it. But there was this one girl—Abigail—she always had to go the extra mile.'

'You shouldn't let it bother you, not now. That was a long time ago.'

Zoe turned her attention to her tuna and ate another mouthful before she answered. 'She said the only reason anyone would want to be friends with me was because it made them look better when they stood beside me.'

Damien wanted to say something conciliatory, but the memory of his own prejudice was lodged in his throat, preventing him. Hadn't he thought something similar? Not that nasty, of course, but he hadn't been able to help comparing the two friends and judging them on their differences.

Sara did seem to shine even brighter next to Zoe, but that wasn't Zoe's fault. Or Sara's.

He put down his knife and fork and looked directly at her. 'You and I both know that nothing is further from the truth in Sara's case.'

Zoe lifted her chin even higher and looked back at him. 'I know,' she said quietly.

But deep down somewhere she hadn't recovered from that comment, Damien realised. What must that be like? To always be cast as second best or, even worse, the 'ugly one'? He'd never known comparisons like that. He'd been an only child and the golden boy at school, the one who went after what he wanted and got it.

The mood had grown far too serious. He decided to use one of Zoe's well-known tactics to lighten things up: he reached over with his fork and stole a juicy chunk of tuna.

'Hey!'

He refused to look repentant. She could take it as well as she dished it out, could she? He wasn't so sure. But, even if she couldn't, it was good to see the fire back in her eyes as she retaliated by stealing a chip from his plate, one eyebrow arched saucily high.

\* \* \*

After dinner they walked back down the endless cobbled steps to the marina. Once back on board *Dream Weaver,* Zoe flopped onto one of the long padded benches in the main cabin, winced and sat back up again.

'Need more of that aftersun?' he asked, and headed off to retrieve it from one of the small lockers above the bench he'd be using as a berth later on before she could answer.

Zoe nodded and took the tube gratefully from him. She then spent a few minutes gently patting the cooling gel into the reddened skin at the tops of her shoulders.

'You have to be careful out on the water,' he said.

Zoe glanced over her shoulder and gave him a sharp look. 'I was careful. I was covered top to toe in sunblock.'

He squashed a spike of irritation at her defensiveness. Couldn't this woman discuss anything without turning it into a fight?

'I wasn't saying you did anything wrong,' he added carefully. 'It's just that somehow the sea and the wind have a way of magnifying the sun's intensity. It can catch you out.'

'Now he tells me,' she muttered as she contorted

her arm behind her head in order to reach her shoulder blades. 'You couldn't have mentioned that up on deck earlier?'

Damien took a step forward. No way was she making this his fault.

'I had no idea you'd burn so quickly and, if you remember, my attention was taken up with sailing a boat single-handed.'

'Well, bully for you!' she snapped, her face contorting as sore skin rubbed against sore skin when she tried to reach a spot in the centre of her back.

'Oh, for goodness' sake! Here… Let me.'

And, without asking, he tugged the tube from her other hand and dumped some of the clear blue gel into his palm.

She went very still, but flinched slightly as the chilly gel met the hot skin of her shoulders. Damien rubbed it in as gently as he could, using just the pads of his fingers, taking his time, making sure he didn't miss even a spot. After a little while, Zoe let out a small whimper and he paused, hands millimetres above her skin.

'Am I hurting you?'

'N…no,' she replied, her voice wavering somewhat.

'Sure?'

She nodded.

Damien looked at the wide elasticated band that made up the bodice of Zoe's garish dress. It rested just below her shoulder blades and prevented further progress.

'Do you want me to do…' he swallowed; all the saliva had drained out of his mouth, as if the tide had gone out there too '…lower down.' He was sure her swimming costume—not that he'd been looking, of course—had dipped lower than that at the back.

Zoe didn't answer for a few seconds. 'Erm…if you could.'

He gently hooked the elastic with one of his non-gooey fingers and lifted it away and down, revealing more tomato-red skin beneath. 'You did a really good job with that sunburn, didn't you?'

He saw her ribs move as she breathed out a little laugh. 'Well, yes, that's me. Never do anything by halves.'

He smiled, even though she couldn't see him. 'I think I've worked that out for myself already.'

He felt rather than heard the shallow chuckle that followed. And then he was quiet again, concentrating on fingers and skin, gel sliding over muscles.

That was one thing Zoe had over skinny girls—she had a nice back. It dipped in invitingly in the middle, no ribs or bones protruding, and it was all curves and soft skin, no sharp contours. He let his fingers and palms gently skim each one.

And then he realised that he'd run out of gel, and for the last minute or so he'd just been lost in following his eyes with his fingers. Exploring.

He wasn't supposed to be exploring. He was just supposed to be helping.

He pulled his hands away and very gently replaced the gathered section of Zoe's dress back where it was supposed to be, ignoring the inviting drip of gel on the end of the tube that was just begging to be used up.

She turned to face him, her hands at the front of her dress, where they'd clutched the fabric to keep it from sliding down. Her eyes were big and her lips slightly parted. It reminded him of how she'd looked in the moonlight the night before.

Had that really been less than twenty-four hours ago? It felt more like a decade. At least he felt he'd aged that much since then.

But thinking about the…incident…by the fountain made him realise he'd been remiss. There were things he should have said that he hadn't.

'I'm sorry,' he said and, before he could continue, Zoe jumped in.

'Don't be. My back feels much better now.'

'No,' he said, thinking he really should take a step back, move away. 'I meant about last night… About kissing you the way I did.'

That left Zoe silent and blinking. Not a very common sight.

'I…' She fell silent again, looked down at her brightly painted toenails.

'It wasn't a very gentlemanly thing to do.'

'No, it wasn't,' she replied but, instead of her voice being hard and confrontational as he'd expected it to be, it was low and husky.

'You had every right to slap me. I think I needed it.' He puffed out some air and ran his hand through his hair. 'Let's just say that I wasn't at my best that day, for a whole string of reasons I don't really want to go into.'

She didn't say anything else, just searched his face with her eyes. He felt as if he was an interesting specimen on a microscope slide. She was looking at him as if she'd seen nothing quite like it before.

'Thank you.' Her voice was steady and low. 'I've done plenty of things in the heat of the moment

I've had to apologise for later, so I know what the genuine article is when it comes my way.' Her lips curved into the barest of smiles and he saw the sparkle of something warm and soft and gentle in the backs of her eyes. 'I appreciate that, Damien.'

He nodded.

He still hadn't stepped away, he realised. Now would be a really good time. Before he did *two* things he needed to apologise for within twenty-four hours.

Zoe's hands were still clutching the front of her dress, but she dropped them now and held one of them out to him. 'Truce?'

He slid his hand into hers and they shook solemnly. 'Truce.'

Then something occurred to him. 'Wait a minute... Didn't we declare a truce of sorts this morning?'

The softness, the vulnerability was gone now and the impish Zoe was back. 'Technically, yes, but it didn't count,' she said as she withdrew her hand from his and looked at it. 'Yuck.'

Damien mirrored her. He'd forgotten that blobs of gel still clung to the edges of his hands. 'And why didn't it count?' he asked, still staring at his palm.

She lifted her arm. 'Because I was lying.'

And then she dragged her palm across his face, wiping the excess gel off on his cheek, before grinning saucily at him and disappearing into the cabin. He stood there, his gaze alternating between his upturned palm and the cabin door.

He had a feeling he'd just become friends with Zoe St James.

Sara and Luke would be delighted. But Damien? He wasn't sure whether he should be pleased that the war was over or just very, very scared.

# CHAPTER SEVEN

WHILE the good weather continued Zoe spent a lot of time during the next few days in the sunshine, even though she made sure she was covered up. She either lounged up the front of the boat while Damien managed things down at the business end, or window shopped on her own in the little towns they visited, looking at girly things such as shoes and pretty locally made trinkets.

She wasn't avoiding Damien. They'd agreed to have separate holidays, hadn't they? And they met up each evening to go out to dinner. It was all very grown-up and civilised.

They discussed cooking on board, but Damien's utilitarian menu ideas, involving limited rations, had Zoe screwing her face up, and Zoe's more flamboyant suggestions put a look of fear in Damien's eyes. Eating out solved the problem. No fighting about food then, because they could choose what they wanted, but Zoe made sure she kept her grubby mitts off Damien's plate now.

Somehow that had become dangerous territory. Mainly because it reminded her of what had happened *after* that meal. She couldn't quite look that tube of aftersun in the face any more.

She wandered along the narrow streets of Fowey on one of her daily shopping trips, and stopped to stare into a smart but quirky jewellery shop window. Just the memory of that massage had her placing a palm on the window to steady herself. She fanned her face down with her non-supporting hand and heaved in a breath.

Okay, so Damien wasn't quite the arrogant snob she'd pegged him for, but that didn't mean that having the hots for him was a good idea. He was still the same type as her ex-fiancé, and that kind of man wanted a certain kind of woman in his life, even if he said he didn't. And if there was one thing that Zoe had taken away from the whole call-off-the-wedding-because-I'm-in-love-with-someone-else fiasco, it was that she wasn't that kind of woman.

She sighed as she looked at her reflection in the shop window. One side of her face was a little more tanned than the other now, but it was almost back to normal. Nothing a little tinted moisturiser couldn't cope with.

It still pained her to think of her time with Aiden. Not so much because she'd lost the man, but more the loss of the fairy tale he'd brought with him. She'd never thought someone as wonderful as him would ever be interested in someone like her. It was as if Prince Charming has swooned at the raggedy Cinderella's feet instead of waiting until she'd got all dolled up for the ball. She'd never felt so wanted.

But somehow the story had gone into reverse. The clock had stuck midnight, the prince took one look at Cinders, had suddenly seen the rags for what they were, and had run a mile in the other direction. With one week to go before the wedding.

She looked at her reflection in the shop window again, looked herself steadily in the eye. *So no more thinking about getting deliberately sunburnt just to be on the receiving end of Damien's magic fingers again, okay?*

She nodded back at herself just as sternly.

That settled, she peeled her hand from the window and went inside to have a look round. The shop was tucked into the ground floor of a row of Georgian buildings, compact but beautifully decorated. The wood panelling had been painted off-white and the silver and amber jewellery the shop specialised in was housed in glass cases that lined the walls. A bit restrained for Zoe's tastes, maybe, but it showed the pieces off beautifully.

She always liked to see other designers' work and she spent ages browsing, but she found herself admiring the shop more than its contents. One day she'd have one of these. A nice little quirky shop with a workshop at the back and a comfy little corner where she could talk to clients about designing bespoke pieces. Selling her designs to other shops around south-east England was all well and good and she was starting to make a name for herself, but it would be really lovely to have a shop of her own. One day…

She made it back to the marina at about twenty to six. Damien had said to be back by five, but she'd spent much longer in that shop than she'd meant to. She walked down the ramp and on to the pontoons, but when she came to the spot where *Dream Weaver* had been moored she found a large, sparkling cruiser.

She rested her hands on her hips, causing her paper shopping bags to fan out around her. Where the heck had he gone? She carried on to the end of the pontoon and stared out across the water.

All the while she'd been standing there, the buzz

of an outboard motor had been getting louder and louder somewhere close by. A flash of sunlight on the water drew her attention, and that was when she saw him—Damien—coming towards her in a little grey inflatable dinghy. He wasn't looking very happy.

Zoe put both hands behind her back in an attempt to make a shopping trip seem slightly less successful. Why did these little boutiques have to wrap everything in tissue paper and put it in an oversized bag, anyway?

Don't react, she told herself as he brought the dinghy round to the end of the pontoon and slipped its rope round a bollard.

'I said *five*,' he shouted over the noise of the engine.

Zoe bestowed her most fetching smile on him. 'What's a few minutes when we've got ten whole days to fill?'

It didn't work. He just glowered back.

'I explained that these were short-stay berths, that we only had two hours and that we needed to move to a swinging mooring by five.'

He well might have. But after thirty seconds of sailing jargon it all started sounding like *blah, blah, blah* to Zoe.

'What's the rush, anyway?'

Damien remained stony-faced as she handed the first of her shopping bags to him.

'Hey!' she said as he chucked them unceremoniously into the triangular space at the front of the dinghy, just forward of the little inflatable seat.

He held out a hand so she could steady herself climbing in, but Zoe needed both arms to keep the rest of her bags out of his clutches. She managed somehow without his help and sat abruptly down on the little bolster-shaped seat, facing him.

Damien eyed the brightly coloured bags before casting off. 'How many pairs of flip-flops does one woman need, anyway?' he muttered as he reversed away from the pontoon then swung the dinghy round to plough across the river against the current. 'If we want to get into town by seven-thirty to eat, we need to get the food shopping done by six forty-five, and I couldn't take the dinghy to do that until I'd picked you up.'

'Sorry,' Zoe said softly. She hadn't been late on purpose, just had got caught out in a little day-dreaming. 'Can't we just shop a bit quicker or go into town a bit later?' Seriously, would the earth fall from its axis if they weren't sitting down and ordering by eight?

Damien didn't answer, so obviously it would.

*Dream Weaver* was about five minutes away, secured to a mooring buoy up a large creek near a wooded part of the riverbank, away from the noise and bustle of the marina. Damien didn't bother turning the engine off when they reached her, but let Zoe climb aboard while he held the dinghy steady. She had to post her bags through the railings into the cockpit before climbing up the ladder at the back of the boat. Once her foot was on the first rung, he was off again, speeding away in the direction of the town centre and the supermarket.

Heaven forbid the boat wasn't stocked with exactly three tins or packets of everything on Damien's shopping list at all times. He really was quite neurotic about it. But then Zoe went to make herself a cup of tea and discovered they were out of milk, and she couldn't even moan about it because she was the one who'd finished it off.

It was quiet in this spot and there was no one else to talk to, as there would have been at the marina, so Zoe reached into one of her shopping bags and pulled out a beautiful leather-bound sketchpad she just hadn't been able to resist. She then rummaged for a pencil in the navigation desk before returning to the cockpit and settling down to draw.

But she didn't draw the scenery. Well, not exactly…

She took the shape, the textures of the landscape, and turned them into designs for bracelets and earrings and necklaces. Rolling hills and soft clouds, clean sharp lines and rippling water were stylised and shaped into silver.

Ever since she'd designed Sara's ring she'd started to think about doing something different, more understated. She'd wanted to find a theme to tie some of the new collection together, and now it seemed she had it. She was so engrossed in what she was doing that she only noticed Damien had returned when a plastic carrier bag full of bread and apples came over the side of the boat and landed on the bench beside her. She put her pencil and pad down, flipping the pad closed first, and went to help.

She supposed she could have gone shopping with him, but that would have defeated the object of 'separate holidays'. Anyway, Damien didn't seem to like to sit still and Zoe did—rather a lot—especially when she was on holiday, so she decided not to stop him if he'd silently volunteered for the job.

She put the kettle on and made Damien a cup of tea. They'd got into a semi-comfortable routine over the last couple of days, working around each other, doing their own thing, talking only when they needed to. It was working. Sort of.

Damien bounded down the cabin steps with the last of the shopping, looking far too strong and healthy for Zoe's liking, in a soft cotton T-shirt and knee-length shorts. He gladly accepted the tea she offered and took it back outside into the sunshine.

Zoe knew she ought to stay in the cabin, not go out and join that six-foot hunk of male healthiness sitting outside, all wind-ruffled and glowing from his jaunt back across the river. But it was such a glorious day... And it was ever so dingy in the tiny cabin, with only those long thin windows high up in the wall to let in light.

She emerged into the cockpit to find Damien sipping his tea and flipping through her sketchbook.

'Hands off, nosey,' she said, attempting to swat his hand away from it.

Damien didn't have any trouble fending her off,

even with a cup of tea in one hand. 'A very different style for you—even from Sara's ring—which I thought was beautiful, by the way.'

She stopped her ineffectual swatting. 'Thank you…I think.'

He looked up at her, a mischievous glint in his eye. 'You think?'

Zoe fidgeted. 'Well, in my experience, it pays to be wary of compliments from good-looking men—' She stopped and blushed.

Damien's glint worked its way from his eyes down to his mouth. 'In my experience, it pays to compliment attractive women.'

Zoe, who'd been half-enjoying the gentle banter, despite her mortification, suddenly snatched her pad out of his hands and retreated to the cabin door. 'Don't make fun of me, Damien,' she said, her voice hard on the surface while her stomach quivered underneath.

'I wasn't. I was just—'

She didn't wait to hear the rest. She turned and headed back down inside and tucked the sketchbook safely away in her cabin. Then she folded her legs underneath herself and sat on her bunk.

She didn't want Damien to say things like that to her. It would make the raging crush she seemed to be developing for him *so* much harder to control. In fact, she thought she preferred it when they were bickering. At least then she was safe.

Without stopping to think whether it was a good idea or not, she stood on the bunk, opened the hatch in the roof of her cabin and stuck her head through it.

'Next time you can keep your opinions to yourself,' she yelled in the direction of the cockpit. 'About me or my work. Separate holidays, remember?'

And then she flopped down on her bunk, leaving the hatch open as ventilation.

There. He wouldn't think she was very attractive after the way she'd screwed her face up and yelled at him, and that was fine by her. She didn't need another smooth man who was way out of her league, giving her hope, making her believe in herself before whipping it all away from her again.

Remember what he's like, she told herself, when he's not in shorts and a T-shirt, when he looks all buttoned-up and rigid, not relaxed like this. That's the real Damien Stone and you'd better not forget it.

But then a shadow blocked out the sun momentarily and a soft thud on the sleeping bag beside her completely undermined her resolve. He'd finished unpacking the shopping, it seemed. Found a bag she'd missed.

A small bar of her favourite chocolate sat innocently on the bunk with a Post-it note attached. *For emergencies*, it said in a strong, dark scrawl.

Damn that man, Zoe thought, as she ripped the foil open and sunk her teeth into it. She didn't want him to be nice to her, not when she was doing her best to put him off, because she was starting to like—really like—Damien Stone. And if that wasn't an emergency, she didn't know what was.

Zoe woke the following morning to find a huge grey cloud hanging over her cabin skylight. She did her usual contortionist's act to get dressed in the tiny triangular space. Maybe sharing it with a huge case hadn't been such a great idea after all.

When she emerged, most annoyed at having to put something with long sleeves on, she found Damien humming to himself in the little galley, cooking sausages and looking horrendously chirpy. Didn't he know that grey skies on a holiday practically required one to be in a state of mourning?

She yawned. Zoe wasn't usually an early riser but the daylight flooding into her cabin and the noise of the wire shrouds banging against the top of the mast in the wind had been a pretty effective alarm clock.

'Where are we off to today?' she mumbled as Damien shoved a mug of tea in her direction.

'Mevagissey,' he said, and carried on whistling.

'Really? I thought we'd stay here if the weather was going to be bad.'

He made a scoffing noise and looked up to the monochrome sky above the hatch. 'This isn't bad weather. It's not even raining, and the forecast says it'll hold off until evening.'

Zoe leaned forward to follow his gaze. By the looks of that cloud, it would rain sooner rather than later.

'It's perfect sailing weather,' Damien announced matter-of-factly.

Well, they obviously had very different ideas about what perfect sailing involved. If it didn't involve a cool drink and a bikini, Zoe didn't want to know.

'You've got a waterproof coat with you, haven't you?' he asked, looking a little concerned.

Zoe rolled her eyes. 'Of course.' Even she wasn't that stupid. This was an English summer, after all.

Damien seemed to have inhaled his sausage sandwich while she'd been staring heavenwards and grumbling about the weather, and now he glugged the last of his tea down and bounded up top with all the restraint of a springer spaniel.

Zoe slid forward onto the table until her cheek met polished wood and then stared at her mug with one eye. Damien had better be right about this perfect day of sailing ahead, otherwise he might just have a mutiny on his hands.

The wind sliced through Damien's hair, lifting it at its roots, and he turned his face to the wind. *Dream Weaver* was listing about forty-five degrees, her sails full, and he stood with one foot on the sloping cockpit floor, the other on the lee-ward bench and both hands on the tiller.

As he'd told Zoe—perfect sailing weather. They were making fabulous progress. In fact, if they kept this up they might even make the Scillies a day early. And if there was one thing Damien liked better than sticking to the plan, it was being one step ahead of the plan.

Thinking of Zoe… Where was she? He hadn't

seen her since he'd hoisted the sails and cut the motor, and that had been over an hour ago. She was missing all the fun.

'Zoe?' he yelled in the direction of the hatch. He'd go and find her, but the wind had been steadily increasing in force and he needed both hands to hang on to things. In fact, an extra pair of hands would be a godsend. He opened his mouth to yell again. 'Zo—'

A dishevelled copper head appeared in the hatchway. The face, however, was grey and her eyes were huge. He'd never noticed before that they weren't brown but a more woody olive-green. Unfortunately, the ashy colour of her complexion was bringing the colour out nicely.

'Not feeling too hot, I take it.'

She shook her head and turned to go back inside.

'You'd be better out here,' he added.

Slowly, she twisted back to look at him, her disbelief obvious.

'No, really. It's just like being car sick. Keeping an eye on the horizon and plenty of fresh air will help.'

She stayed where she was for a second, but then continued up the steps. It was then that he realised her waterproof coat had some kind of animal print on it—in luminous pink, for goodness' sake. He knew he shouldn't, not when she was feeling so rough, but he couldn't help himself. He had to fake a cough so he could cover his mouth and hide his smile. There was nothing predictable about Zoe St James.

Once in the cockpit, she shuffled over to one of the benches and turned as if to sit down and huddle in the corner. Before she could do so, he grabbed hold of her and positioned her on the other side of the tiller. 'Here, hold this,' he said, and shoved it into her hands. 'I just need to check on something.'

Zoe let out a strangled noise which could have been a scream, and the boat lurched as she lost control for a moment. Damien, however, had learned his lesson from the first day on board *Weaver* with Zoe, and was hanging on to one of the shrouds that ran from the deck to support the mast.

She needed something to do, something to keep her mind off feeling so queasy—and he could use the help when it was blowy like this.

'Hold it steady,' he shouted back, meeting her

wide eyes with his own focused gaze and noting the thin line of her mouth.

'But I don't know what I'm doing,' she shouted back. The last word was muffled somewhat when a clump of ginger curls landed in her mouth.

'You're doing fine,' he said. 'Just hold her steady. See that radio mast up on the cliffs?'

She spat her hair out of her mouth and nodded gravely.

'Just keep aiming for that. I'll be back with you in a second.'

He did what he needed to do but, once back in the cockpit, he stayed just far enough away to prevent Zoe handing the tiller back to him. She was looking better already. He just had to keep her concentrating on something other than her head and her stomach.

'Now you're here, I could do with some help. I want to change the direction of the boat. If we keep going on this course we won't end up where we want to.'

Zoe squinted at him. 'Can't we just point the boat in the direction we want to go?'

Damien opened his mouth to give a mini-lecture on the subject, but then had second thoughts. He jumped down beside Zoe. 'Try it. Move the tiller in the opposite direction to where you want to go: left to turn right, or right to turn left.' He pointed to the south-west, where the little harbour town of Mevagissey awaited them. Tentatively, she gave the polished wooden tiller a push and was rewarded with a slight change of course. When she was happy with that, she tried again, bolder this time, and *Dream Weaver* turned into the wind.

Immediately the mainsail deflated like a let-down party balloon and the jib flapped wildly. The yacht began to slow, no longer pushing through the waves.

'Oh...' said Zoe, suddenly looking very worried. 'What did I do?'

Damien smiled. 'Don't worry. That always happens when you turn the boat into the wind. The sails can't catch any of it. So when our destination is the same direction as the wind, we have to tack—or make a zigzagging path—sailing with the wind on one side and then the other.'

Zoe looked up at the flapping mainsail. 'Oh, I get it. So I just need to push this thing a bit—'

'Hold on.' Damien reached out and grabbed the tiller, steadying it with his hand. 'See this sail at the front? It's called the jib. If we're going to tack now we have to loosen the ropes that hold it in—the sheets…' he noted Zoe's raised eyebrows '…I'll explain later. We have to loosen the sheet on one side and tighten it on the other, so the jib can move over to the other side of the boat. You can help me winch.'

Zoe's cheeks were flushed pink now and the dullness had gone out of her eyes. 'Okay,' she said, smiling slightly. 'Holding ropes…I can do that.'

'Just do what I say and you'll be fine.'

She let out a dry laugh. 'Ah, so that's what this is all about! I bet you can sail this boat with just your little finger. This is your excuse to order me around.'

'Chance would be a fine thing,' he replied.

But she paid attention and followed instructions all afternoon as they criss-crossed the bay. At one point he handed the tiller back to her, pointing out the compass heading she needed to stick to, and she actually grinned at him.

'How do you know all of this stuff, exactly what to do?' she asked. 'Are there hard and fast rules, tables and numbers to learn?'

'Partly,' he said, leaning back against the cabin wall and watching her handling the tiller with confidence now. 'But you never know exactly what's going to happen until you get out on the water. No two sailing days are identical, and that's half the fun of it—pitting yourself against the wind and the waves, making it to your destination despite the obstacles, knowing that you were ultimately in control of these unpredictable forces, making them work for you rather than against you.'

Zoe frowned a little, but one side of her mouth curled up. 'Who are you and what have you done with the real Damien Stone?'

He stopped smiling. What did she mean by that?

'Oh, come on…' Zoe said, chuckling slightly. 'You? Going with the flow, dealing with the unpredictable? Doesn't really sound like you, does it?'

'Then you don't know me very well,' he said, and looked out over the grey waves. 'When you're sailing you have to be flexible, and I can be as flexible as the next guy.'

Zoe's guffaw had him snapping his head back round to look at her. 'If the next guy is a tin soldier, maybe…'

Damien stood up straight. 'I think you're making a rather sweeping statement.'

She sighed. 'Damien, I have never met anyone

as structured as you. You have a plan for every-thing.'

'Not everything,' he mumbled. Not really. He hadn't planned to come on this holiday with Zoe St James, had he?

She did that thing with her eyebrows again. 'Oh, no? So what time are we supposed to be sailing into Mevagissey harbour?'

He shuffled a little, then took the tiller back from her. 'Three-thirty…if the wind stays like this.'

'Exactly,' Zoe said softly, and then she walked to the edge of the cockpit, rested her hands on the side of the boat and stared out towards the cliff. 'But what if we decided we wanted to take a de-tour?'

Damien pressed his lips together. Detour? What sort of detour? There was nowhere else to go.

Zoe was smiling at him. He didn't like that smile.

'There's a beautiful beach over there—totally deserted. Can we go and have a look?'

Everything inside Damien stiffened, and he knew that Zoe saw every muscle fibre snap to attention. He could tell it from the way that an-noying little smile grew even more asymmetrical.

'You can't cope with it, can you?' she said, her voice almost a whisper, her eyes sparkling. 'Admit it.'

He was admitting nothing. He'd spoken the truth earlier on. Sailing required a man to be flexible, yes, but a sailor was always in control of the decisions—when to sail, when to stay in port, which sails to use, what compass heading to go on. And if he wanted to he could choose to go and visit a beach he'd never even noticed before, even if he'd been sailing these waters for more than ten years. Just because he'd got into the habit of focusing on that mast on the headland, it didn't mean he couldn't do things differently this time.

He pulled the tiller towards him and let *Dream Weaver's* sails out as the boat turned and the wind came full-on from the port side. And, with one last longing look at that spike of metal on the hill and with the sensation of a ticking stopwatch inside his chest, Damien pulled hard on the tiller and headed off to the strip of yellow where sea met cliff.

# CHAPTER EIGHT

THEY eventually made it to the harbour village of Mevagissey, so pretty it featured on many a 'Greetings from Cornwall' postcard. The old fishing port filled a sheltered valley and was further protected by a sturdy harbour wall. The houses had spread beyond the narrow streets and up the surrounding hillside so they seemed to perch on top of each other, all vying for the best view of the bay.

'The joys of sailing, huh?' Zoe said. Her fuchsia leopard-print rain mac was plastered to her head and was making her feel very sweaty, which was no mean feat, considering it had condescended to put up with ten minutes of rain and spray before giving up and letting any moisture that landed on it in.

Damien was tying a rope round a cleat on the quay. He jumped back on board *Dream Weaver* in one smooth motion. 'If I remember rightly, it was your idea to take a "detour". We might have been here by the time the weather hit otherwise.'

Yes, there was that. But she wasn't going to tell him that sticking to the plan might have been a good idea after all. That would undo all the good work she'd done that afternoon.

And what a detour it had been! Something new to experience, all right, but not exactly what Zoe had been expecting. Oh, the beach had been fun—while the weather had lasted. They'd dropped anchor a short way away and had taken the dinghy to the shore. Then they'd walked along a virgin beach that may not have seen another human footprint in months, thanks to the remote location. Even Damien had looked as if he was enjoying himself—which had been part of *her* plan. Mr Live-by-the-timetable needed to learn how to loosen up a little, stop and smell the roses, and Zoe had decided that she was the one to teach him. It was a fair exchange for teaching her how to sail.

But the pearly bright sky had changed within ten minutes of landing. It was as if that dark cloud she'd seen that morning had been stalking them, staying out of sight until it had its chance to pounce.

Damien had told her repeatedly that it wasn't a gale and they were perfectly safe, but she felt as if, just as he'd said in his rather impressive speech, they'd pitted themselves against wind and waves on the journey into Mevagissey. Pity that the final score had been elements one, humans zero. She didn't think she remembered ever being so wet and cold.

She would have added *miserable* to the list, but she had a horrible feeling she'd almost enjoyed helping Damien sail *Dream Weaver* to her destination. Despite the hair plastered to her face and a coat with a hood that was so useless it didn't matter if it was up or down, an adrenalin surge had warmed her insides. Or maybe that had been the quiet look of approval on Damien's face every time he'd caught her eye.

Blast that rain cloud. She'd have been safer if she could have kept out of his way and sunbathed as normal.

And blast Damien Stone for being right again. Not following the rules—the handed-down wisdom of generations—would have been disastrous in all that wind and rain, she could see that now. Not the time for reacting from her gut, but for thinking ahead, doing as she was told. None of her friends would have believed their eyes if they'd seen her. She'd moaned long and hard about the weather conditions to compensate, though. Now *that* was more like the Zoe St James everyone knew and loved.

'Well, Master and Commander of the ocean,' she said in a droll tone, casting a look in Damien's direction. 'I'm off to get warm and dry and clean.' And then she hauled her aching limbs down the stairway and into her cabin.

She bundled herself into the tiny little shower-slash-bathroom and scrubbed and soaped until her body was no longer tired and achy, until she smelled of something other than damp clothes and salt. By the time she got dressed again she started to feel more human, which meant she was more likely to act like it. Always a good thing.

Zoe emerged from her cabin just as Damien was pulling on a clean sweatshirt. The sight of a lightly tanned and muscled back sent all the words she'd had ready to say flittering out of her head. He must have heard her because he turned round suddenly and looked at her.

'Hi,' she said. Obviously one word—a very basic one—had decided not to desert her. She was very grateful to it. Then another one came back to roost. 'Sorry,' she added.

His eyebrows raised. And was that the start of a smile she could see at the corners of his mouth? She couldn't tell.

'For moaning on and on about the weather,' she added. 'I get a little tetchy when I'm soaked to the skin.'

He blinked and his face remained totally deadpan. 'You do surprise me.'

Zoe felt a little bubble of laughter rise up in her throat. She hiccuped and let it out. 'Never been known to suffer in silence, me,' she said, smiling a little. 'But with four older brothers who liked to use me for wrestling practice, there's a reason for that.'

Damien nodded and shrugged. 'I'm an only child, so I wouldn't know about wrestling or brothers. I'll take your word for it.'

Ah, of course he was. She could see it now—that telltale air of entitlement and confidence that could only come from being the apple of Mummy and Daddy's eye. Unlike Zoe, who had been an unplanned late addition to her clan of sport-loving, high-achieving brothers. Her mother always used to joke that she hadn't known what to do with a girl after all those boys, and Zoe reckoned it had showed. She'd been the tag-along kid, always trailing after her brothers to their different sports matches, always standing in their much larger shadows.

'I can teach you a few good headlocks if you want.'

She'd started talking in a jaunty voice, just making a joke to cover things over the way she always did, but by the end of the sentence her mind had flipped away from wrestling matches on the living room carpet to having her arms wound round Damien, exploring that fine back she'd just had a glimpse of, and in her daydream they definitely *weren't* wrestling. Her voice trailed away and she realised the extra layer of clothes she'd put on had been one too many.

Damien didn't have much to say to that either, so they just stared at each other for a few seconds until he moved towards her, making her jump.

He cleared his throat. 'We need to find you something more practical to wear than that…pink thing.'

Zoe glanced through the high, narrow windows of the cabin at the gloomy sky. It was only late afternoon and on a sunny day it would have been light for hours longer, but today it seemed as if twilight had already cocooned them.

'I could buy something tomorrow, but it doesn't look as if it's going to let up this evening.' She sighed. 'I'm probably going to get drenched all over again on the way to dinner.'

Damien did his own reconnaissance of the sky, frowned, then looked back at her. 'Maybe not,' he said mysteriously, then moved past her to open the cupboard opposite the bathroom. Zoe scampered out of his way, noting that as he'd got close her internal thermostat had risen another couple of notches.

No, she told herself. Not a good idea. He's not for the likes of you.

Damien returned only moments later with a bright yellow jacket on a hanger.

'I remembered Luke and Sara had some spare oilskins in the locker,' he said and handed her the hanger.

Zoe slid the waxy rubber duck-coloured coat on. The arm length was fine, but over the bust? Not even close, matey. She blushed hard and shrugged it off quickly.

What had she been thinking? Of course she wouldn't fit into Sara's coat. She never tried on her friend's clothes any more, remembering the few times she had and knowing that the results in the mirror would mock her. Not a natural clothes horse, was Zoe, because she wasn't as slender as Sara. But then there were a lot of ways she wasn't like Sara. Not as pretty. Not as clever. Not as popular. The list was practically endless.

And now Damien had seen her in Sara's jacket, he wouldn't be able to help making the comparison, just like everybody else did. She looked at the floor as she handed the jacket back to him.

'I'm not sure I'm that hungry, anyway,' she mumbled. 'Maybe a bowl of cereal would do.'

He really should look at her face, not where his gaze had slid and snagged when she'd tried to pull the coat tight across her chest. Heat flooded his torso and it took him a couple of seconds to register what she'd said, but the words finally filtered through. Move your eyes *now*, Damien, before she looks up and catches you staring where you shouldn't.

He managed it just in time. A split second later Zoe's focus flicked from the wooden floor to his face and then back again.

She had no idea, did she? Absolutely no idea

that she'd brought him to a gibbering standstill, that she'd drained all his willpower away, making him question whether following through on the unacknowledged attraction between them would really be as catastrophic as he'd first thought. She wasn't his type at all.

His body begged to disagree.

He told his body to shut up.

Damien was used to taking control of every urge that was counterproductive to his grand life goals, and he squashed this one down alongside all the others. Pity he didn't notice that, just like an overstuffed ship's locker, there was hardly any more room in that place where he stuffed all those whims and desires and dreams he didn't like. Things were starting to bulge out. One day soon the lid might just pop off, exhausted from keeping all those pesky things at bay.

'What if I went out and brought back some take-away?'

There was another one of those rogue urges now. It slid free and hit him between the eyes just as Zoe looked up at him from under her lashes and bit her lip.

*Kiss it*, the urge said. *Taste that lip—bite it, even.*

'You'd do that for me?' she said quietly.

He nodded emphatically. Air. Space. Those were things he needed in large quantities at present. And a cold shower, courtesy of the English summer, probably wouldn't hurt.

'What do you want?' he said, backing away, pretending he was reaching for his jacket. 'Fish and chips? Pizza?'

He saw the gratitude in her eyes, and a third jolt hit him.

No. That shouldn't have happened. This was only supposed to be a physical attraction. It wasn't supposed to happen when she looked all soft and vulnerable and un-Zoe-like for a few seconds.

But he needn't have worried. She offered him a reprieve. Seconds later the softness left her, replaced by an over-bright smile and animated hand gestures as she talked.

'You're forgetting there's one more coat in the cupboard,' she said, grinning at him. 'One that shouldn't find my physique so much of a challenge.' And before he could stop her she pushed her way into the little upright locker and had re-emerged with Luke's oilskin. She threw it on and zipped it up, battling with sleeves that were easily four inches too long, and finished it off by but-

toning her hood up under her chin. Not a flatter-
ing look for anyone.

'I hear pregnant banana is in this season,' she
said, giving a little twirl. And then she'd stuffed
her feet into her trainers and headed for the hatch.
'Come on, you. There's a Korai Chicken in this
town with my name on it somewhere.'

Damien had no choice but to shrug his coat on
and follow. He wanted to reach out and stop her
as she bounced along the quay in the direction of
the high street. Don't do that, he wanted to say.
Don't make a joke of yourself and turn that biting, acidic humour inwards.

The clear, damp air hit Damien's nostrils and
he breathed it in deeply as he followed Zoe into
the heart of Mevagissey.

That was what she did, didn't she? Used that ra-
pier humour of hers not only as a weapon but as
a shield. A very cunning approach. People were
usually too busy licking their wounds after a bout
with Zoe to look too hard at their attacker, to notice the wounds that went wider and deeper in her.

Underneath all that brashness, Zoe St James
was as defenceless as an urchin without its shell,
and she used her quick brain and her creativity

brilliantly to make sure nobody ever guessed the truth.

As they trudged the narrow streets looking for a curry house, Damien began to wonder who'd put those wounds there and how long they'd bled.

He realised now that Zoe was at her snappiest, funniest and most irritating in his presence. It had been her default position with him since almost the first day they'd met, and he started to wonder what on earth he could have done to raise her alarm to maximum alert. What was it about him in particular that set her defences mile-high?

It was as if the weather had decided to apologise for its bad manners the next morning, rewarding them with a day that was as bright and clear as it was warm and breezy. Damien suggested setting out early, trying to round Lizard Point before the day was out, and Zoe didn't disagree for once, slightly repentant and willing to let him have his plans and stick to them—at least for one day.

Later in the afternoon the wind dropped significantly, but it gave Damien a chance to do something he'd wanted to do but had held off doing with just the two of them on board. A bigger crew was needed to do this when the wind was stronger, but now he 'could get the spinnaker out.

Zoe followed instructions, helping with the brightly coloured sail on the foredeck, as he dealt with what needed to be done back in the cockpit and winched it up. She was audibly impressed when the wind caught it and took it high above the bow, making it look like a captured parachute. She spent much of the rest of the journey there, sitting with her legs posted through the metal railings at the tip of the boat, dangling towards the water.

Damien stayed in the stern, smiling. He'd known she'd like the rainbow-coloured spinnaker and had actually been glad the wind had dropped enough finally to get it out for her, as a reward for all her hard work the day before, possibly. A week ago he would have expected her to throw a tantrum over the bad weather, but she'd been amazing. She'd followed every instruction he'd given her in the difficult conditions perfectly, and he hadn't had to repeat anything.

The afternoon passed with them at their opposite ends of the boat but, unlike before, when Damien had felt the resistance, like two magnets pushing each other away, it now felt easy. Peaceful. So peaceful, in fact, that Damien was shocked when he looked at his watch and realised time had been slipping away far too quickly.

It was late in the afternoon and he hadn't kept a check on their progress. The silent sense of satisfaction that had paused time that afternoon quickly ebbed away. Rounding the Lizard would take more hours than they had before nightfall. He called Zoe back down from the bow and explained the situation.

'We're going to have to pull into Falmouth and attempt the Lizard tomorrow,' he said as she stepped down into the cockpit, looking windswept.

'That wasn't the plan. Won't it put us behind schedule?'

He kept his face expressionless. 'We've got a new plan now. It's called being flexible. See? I can do it, even without your prompting.'

Why was she laughing? Well, almost laughing. Her eyes were, even if her mouth wasn't.

She turned away and looked towards the large sprawling estuary where three rivers met and merged before pouring into the sea, a jumble of bays and creeks.

'Cool,' she said brightly. 'It looks pretty here.'

So they took down the spinnaker, furled the sails

and motored towards civilisation. Unfortunately, it seemed the rest of Cornwall had decided to converge on Falmouth that weekend—some big regatta was on—and every marina space or mooring was fully booked. They ended up dropping anchor in a sheltered bay on the opposite side of the estuary, just across from the smaller town of St Mawes.

Zoe was ecstatic at their makeshift anchorage for the night. It was a truly beautiful spot. And they'd have missed it, he realised, if they'd powered straight past and headed round the Lizard. Perhaps there was something to be said for detours after all.

The sun was glowing low, just skimming the top of the steep hills, and blistering heat had given way to languid warmth. They were round the tip of the Roseland peninsular, in a sheltered little bay close to a beach. St Mawes, to the north, could be reached easily by the dinghy, and off to the east was a stately home or hotel, its elegant green lawn reaching down to a stone wall at the water's edge.

'Can we swim here?' Zoe asked, practically jumping from foot to foot. 'I feel like a roast chicken and I'm dying for a dip.'

'I don't see why not.'

Zoe squealed and ran below decks, appearing again with all the speed of a quick-change act in a retina-searing multicoloured kaftan thing over the top of her swimming costume.

'Are you coming in?' She reached for the hem of her kaftan and headed for the metal ladder at the stern. 'It's close enough to swim to the beach.'

They were indeed only a hundred feet away, and it was a very pretty little beach. The sea was the other side of the peninsular, but on this side jagged cliffs gave way to a curved green hill, ending with a strip of woodland near the shore. A lone cottage sat between trees and sand, a low, off-white stone building that must have been there for centuries.

However, despite the picturesque surroundings, the beach was almost empty—probably because the layout of the estuary demanded winding roads, and this would be quite a drive from the nearest town with no bridges to speed things up. Only the most determined of beach-hunters would make it this far, leaving the casual holidaymakers to the spots with toilets and cafés and places where they could buy rubber rings and blow-up crocodiles.

Suddenly the thought of that cool water against his sun-baked and salty skin was almost irresistible. 'Give me a minute,' he said, and dived below decks to quickly slip on some swimming shorts.

When he returned, Zoe was nowhere to be seen. He could tell where she was, though, from the series of little shrieks coming from the direction of the ladder.

At the end of the summer the water here would be the warmest it would be all year round, but a heated swimming pool it wasn't. He peered over the railing at the back of the cockpit, grinning, and found Zoe, up to her waist in water, a look of frozen shock on her face.

'Still desperate for that dip?' he asked. 'It'll be better once you're in.'

Zoe just scowled up at him. 'Clear off and let me do it my own way,' she said.

Damien decided that was a very good idea, partly because it could be Christmas before she got off that ladder, and partly because his vantage point was giving him a wonderful view of her cleavage, even though it was encased in a modestly cut one-piece. A figure like Zoe's was impossible to hide. For which he was momentarily very thankful.

But then he remembered all the lectures he'd given himself over the last couple of days. It wouldn't be fair to either of them to start any-thing—well, *continue* what they'd started the night of the wedding—because it just wouldn't go anywhere. They were too different. He knew what kind of woman he wanted: a woman like Sara…

Sara. He realised he'd hardly thought of her in days. Which meant Zoe had, in fact, been doing a fabulous job as a temporary distraction, just as he'd planned. It just wasn't the kind of distraction he'd envisaged. Still, if it was working…

Anyway, since Sara, he'd decided he wasn't going to waste his time dating for the sake of it. Finding the right woman to share his life with was his focus for the moment, and he couldn't—shouldn't—let himself get side-tracked.

In which case, more cold water would definitely help.

He made his way to the side of *Dream Weaver* nearest the beach, climbed over the guard rail and jumped straight in, welcoming the way the chill drove all thoughts of Zoe from his head as he struggled to catch his breath.

# CHAPTER NINE

THEY swam and explored the beach until the sun had almost set. Zoe would have continued to swim there all night if she could have, but Damien suddenly got twitchy, talking about dinner and how busy it would be even in St Mawes, so Zoe reluctantly followed him back to the boat.

He looked so tense by the time they climbed back on board that they just shoved casual clothes on over the top of their swimming things and headed straight off in search of a café or pub in the dinghy.

Just as Zoe had expected, they were fine. They found a pub that served bar snacks and, yes, they had to wait a while for their food and pad the meagre portions out with a couple of packets of crisps, but their tummies were full at the end of the evening, and surely that was what counted?

When she saw Damien scowling at the empty packets, Zoe couldn't help but make an observation. 'You really *don't* like to veer from the plan, do you?'

Damien shrugged as he drained the last of his beer. 'I don't see the crime in that. Plans help you get where you want to go in life.'

She had to give him that. He'd certainly proved that in his professional life.

'You have plans for your business, don't you?' he asked.

Zoe nodded. She had plans, she supposed, although she liked to think of them as dreams. It sounded less suffocating.

'And once you lay down your plans, you start working towards making them a reality, don't you?' Damien added.

Zoe nodded again, although this time she started thinking about her dream of owning her own premises. What exactly *had* she done to make that happen, aside from wandering round other people's shops and sighing? Not a lot, actually.

'But surely there has to be some balance,' she said. 'It can't be work twenty-four hours a day. What about room for fun, the joy that can only come from following a mad impulse?'

Damien's eyes instantly narrowed and his shoulders tensed. When his next words came out, they seemed to have been squeezed out between his teeth. 'What about the chaos that can follow? You were the first one to moan when your "impulse" to divert from the course yesterday afternoon didn't end well.'

'Okay, I admit that, but you have to step outside the box occasionally, follow your heart sometimes?'

Damien pushed his chair back and stood up, even though he hadn't finished his drink. 'That's the problem with people like you. You jump in and "follow your heart"—' he almost sneered as he said those words '—and don't even notice the trail of destruction you leave behind you.'

Zoe smiled, but it was a puzzled smile. What was he talking about? What trail of destruction? Yes, she'd knocked him in the water a few days ago, but apart from that she'd done nothing.

'Nobody said life was perfect. Sometimes it's unpredictable—' her smile grew '—you said it yourself! It's like sailing. Dealing with the unexpected challenges life throws at you, navigating those treacherous times… Aren't those victories the ones that give you the biggest sense of satisfaction in the end?'

Damien shook his head and walked off back towards where the dinghy was moored. 'You don't get it.' There was a hopelessness in his tone that snagged at Zoe's heart, sidetracking the smart reply that had been ready and waiting on her lips.

She followed him in silence until they were back in the little grey inflatable and heading back out across a moonless, glass-smooth bay. He cut the engine as they neared the stern of the boat, letting them float the last few feet, and Zoe stood up and secured the painter to a cleat. She turned to face him, one foot on the ladder, before climbing up on to the yacht.

'Who disappointed you, Damien?' she asked softly. 'So badly that you don't even want to have fun any more?'

He snorted. 'Fun! What good is fun when you've got people who love you, that need you? Pursuing fun like that is selfish…' He seemed to realise he'd said more than he'd meant to and closed his mouth abruptly.

Zoe climbed up the ladder and waited for him in the cockpit, but when Damien climbed on board he walked straight past her, up on to the deck, and sat down on the cabin roof, staring at the oscillating reflections on the water that the vibrations from their outboard motor had caused.

Mad or not, Zoe followed the impulse to go to him. She'd never seen Damien before. And, even though seeing him rattled like this had once been her chief desire, now the moment was here she found it uncomfortable. She climbed out of the cockpit and went and sat next to him. The ridge of the hand rail that ran along the top of the low cabin roof dug into her bottom.

'Who left you behind in their wake of destruction?' she asked, then fell silent. She didn't push, even though she was burning with curiosity.

Night birds that Zoe couldn't name cooed. Gentle ripples, the memory of a boat passing by somewhere else in the estuary, licked the hull. And those shards of reflection had almost mended themselves together again by the time Damien spoke.

'It was my father,' he finally said, his voice strangely scratchy. 'He followed one of those impulsive urges to have fun when I was fifteen, decided to up and leave my mother and I with hardly any warning. He just sat us down at the kitchen table one day, announced he was bored and unfulfilled, and the next day he was gone, off to do something about it.' He turned and looked at her. 'He never came back.'

Zoe laid a hand on Damien's hunched shoulder. 'You didn't ever see him again?' she asked, her voice husky.

Damien blinked slowly and stared back out at the water. 'Oh, I saw him again, but he didn't come home. My mother was heartbroken.'

Zoe swallowed. She didn't have anything to say—smart, sympathetic or otherwise. Instead, she slid her hand along his back and laid her cheek on his shoulder blade.

'So forgive me if I'm not overwhelmed at the idea of following a mad impulse,' Damien added, giving a good impression of Zoe's most sarcastic tone.

She nodded against his back. 'Did he ever find what he was looking for, your father?'

Damien laughed. A low, heartbreaking sound. 'I think he's still looking. That was the funny thing…' He turned to look at her and Zoe peeled her face from his warm cotton shirt and looked back at him. Their faces were close now, only inches away.

'He had a good job, a wife who adored him and ran around after him doing everything she could to make him happy. He had a son who worshipped him. In other words, he had a life many people would kill for. For years I asked myself why it wasn't enough.'

Zoe was finding it a little hard to speak, not only because she was so close to Damien, but because all sense of superiority she'd ever thought she'd seen in his eyes had been stripped away and behind it she only saw pain and defeat.

'Did you ever find any answers?'

Damien nodded and heaved in a deep breath. She saw him start to build the layers of protection back around himself and she wanted to yell out, tell him to stop, but this was the urge she managed to curtail. If anyone understood the need for those layers, it was her.

'My father had unrealistic expectations, for a start. He'd always dreamed of a better life—more money, more social success—and he got to his mid-forties and realised he didn't have what he'd expected he'd have, and he blamed us for it.' He shook his head. 'The stupid thing was that he couldn't see that it was his fault, not ours. He should have worked towards those things instead of just daydreaming about them.'

He gave her a ghostly smile, his teeth shining white in the darkness. 'He should have had a plan.'

Pennies dropped hard and fast inside Zoe's head

now. His father's failure had been a catalyst to Damien's success. She understood now why he was so clear about what he wanted, why he pursued those dreams as if demons were on his tail and, to be honest, she couldn't really blame him for it.

She sighed and joined him in looking out to the little stone cottage on the beach, a fuzzy shape of blue-grey above a strip of silver sand.

'Plans aren't everything,' she said quietly, and heard the same emptiness in her voice that she'd just detected in Damien's. 'Even the best laid ones can backfire and blow up in your face.'

Damien turned to her, and even in the semi-dark she saw the deadness in his eyes had turned back into that one settling, penetrating focus. He trained all of it on her.

'What do you mean?' he asked, and Zoe began to regret that urge to follow him after all.

She shuffled a little, repositioning her well-padded behind on the wooden grab rail. 'I mean that you can plan all you like—dream all you like—but that doesn't mean those things are definitely going to happen.'

Damien's expression told her he'd never even considered such an outrageous notion. 'Such as?'

Zoe shook her head. She didn't want to talk about this. Not with him. Especially now she'd seen under that perfect, polished exterior to the warm, human man beneath. She was already in too much danger; she couldn't let her barriers down as well.

'Zoe?'

She grimaced, her face turned away from him. Her big, fat mouth had got her into hot water again. When would she ever learn?

'You know… Just plans… Things…'

'What sort of things?'

He wasn't going to let this go, was he? And her insides were starting to twitch, to tell her she shouldn't be such a coward, not when he'd opened up to her.

She moved away from him a little, sat up straighter. 'Like weddings…'

'You had a wedding planned?'

His voice was soft and sympathetic, delicious in the anonymous darkness. Could she? Could she confide in this man—a man so like the one who'd broken her heart?

'My love-rat groom phoned one of my bridesmaids from his stag do and confessed his undying love for her.'

There went that mouth of hers again. Really, she was going to have to get herself a muzzle one of these days.

Damien muttered his judgement on her errant fiancé in the form of a rude name.

'Thank you,' Zoe said. And she meant it. Suddenly she was very glad that Damien managed to say and do the right thing ninety-nine per cent of the time. The word had been perfect.

'What about the bridesmaid?' he asked.

Zoe sighed. 'I have better taste in friends than I do in men, it seems. She told him to grow up, and then she did the gutsy thing by coming and telling all to me.'

She leaned back on her hands and stared up at the moonless sky.

'It was a bit of a buzz kill, I can tell you. There was I at the karaoke bar, in full hen night regalia—net curtain veil on a headband, angel wings and L-plates—three verses into "Stand By Your Man". I hogged the mike a bit after that, I'm afraid, Alanis Morrisette being my artiste of choice.'

She let out a little laugh but, instead of floating away on the night air, it seemed to hit the deck.

'You don't have to make a joke out of this, Zoe.'

She breathed in sharply through her nostrils,

furiously ignoring the stinging on the backs of her eyes. 'Actually, I do.'

Hold it in, Zoe. You can't let it all out.

'So, you can see why I'm not big on plans any more,' she added.

Damien swivelled round so he was facing her. 'You don't ever plan to get married or have children? Don't let one loser ruin it for you.'

One loser. Ah, if only there'd been just the one. No, Aiden had merely been the one she was stupid enough to let close enough to hurt her.

'I'm not saying I won't, just that I'm not setting my heart on it. I'll just live my life and see what happens.'

Damien nodded, but his expression told her he couldn't think of anything worse.

'Anyway,' she said, 'this is supposed to be a holiday. It's practically illegal to get maudlin.' She stood up and rubbed the grab rail dent out of her backside. 'I've found that the best way to cheer myself up is to do something new, something unexpected.'

One option was to lean into Damien and seek refuge against his shoulder again. But that would be truly pathetic, especially as he must think her a horribly sad case after her recent revelation.

The only other thing she could think of doing was to pull her cotton jersey sundress over her head, kick off her shoes and jump overboard. And that was exactly what she did.

She'd thought the water would be colder than it had been earlier in the day but, if anything, it felt warmer. Probably something to do with the ambient temperature of the air being closer to that of the water, she thought distantly as her head went under.

She opened her eyes just before she broke the surface again, kicking upwards, and at first nothing made sense. Tiny specks of bluish-green light danced around her. It was as if the stars had dropped out of the sky and had sprinkled themselves on the surface of the water like icing sugar on a cake. She laughed as soon as her mouth was above water, and then spun around, treading water arms outstretched.

'It's magic!' she yelled, feeling like a kid on Christmas morning. What was this? Every time she moved the water sparkled around her, as if she were setting off miniature underwater fireworks. She stopped spinning and swam away from the boat and the lights followed, clinging to her, dancing with her. After a few strokes, she turned and trod water, looked back to the dark shadow sitting on the roof of *Dream Weaver*'s cabin.

'What is this?' she yelled, her voice musical with latent laughter.

The shadow stood up, moved to the edge of the deck. Zoe stopped laughing, closed her mouth and trod water silently. Suddenly she felt very, very serious and she didn't know why.

Damien watched her from the deck. He hadn't planned to stand up; he'd just been drawn to her, had moved closer without even thinking. He couldn't take his eyes off her.

Sara would never have done this—jumped into the sea at night on a whim, relished in the natural phenomenon so totally and completely—and for once he was one hundred per cent glad that this wasn't Sara. This moment was Zoe's, hers and hers alone.

She'd gone still and, even though he couldn't see her face, Damien realised she was watching him, waiting for him to speak. He gave her something better. Something unexpected.

He slipped off the T-shirt he'd thrown on over his long swimming shorts, prised his feet from his deck shoes and joined her.

She screamed as he jumped in, and then she laughed. Not the same kind of sound as a few moments earlier—this one was part shock, part nervousness—but he couldn't help but join her in that also. He didn't think he'd ever swum while laughing before, and he discovered it involved drinking more salt water than he'd wanted to. For some reason, that just made him laugh harder.

The water lit up around him too, linking them long before he reached her.

'It's phosphorescence,' he said between deep breaths when he started to tread water beside her. 'Tiny little bioluminescent marine life forms that react to movement.'

Zoe's eyes grew wide. 'All this? From plankton?'

'Pretty much.' He moved his arm through the water again, just to see them sparkle almost neon green. He'd seen it before, of course, tiny specs of light trailing behind a ship on a dark night sailing, but he'd never got down *into* the water and swum in it before—and he wouldn't have done, if not for Zoe's mad impulse to jump overboard.

She'd called it magic, and while his very logical and practical brain refused such definitions, part of him was starting to agree. Maybe it was the setting: the quiet, secluded bay, the stately home in the distance. Maybe it was the water, so flat that every reflection was perfect.

He stopped watching the bright flecks dancing round his fingers as he used his hands to keep himself afloat and looked at Zoe, totally absorbed in doing the same thing.

Maybe it was this woman.

Maybe she'd brought the magic with her, because he'd seen this phenomenon before but had never felt this sense of wonder.

He turned the next arm movement into a splash, dousing her with water.

She screamed. Loudly. But there was no one here to shush them, so he did it again.

'Right!' she spluttered. 'You've asked for it.'

He discovered Zoe was a worthy opponent. She held nothing back in trying to dunk him under. But his arms were longer, always able to keep her at bay, and without the weight advantage—which she didn't have, no matter how much she moaned about her curves—she had no hope of success.

At least, that was what he thought until she disappeared under the water and didn't emerge again. He searched for her, backing away from the spot where they'd been splashing, hoping the telltale creatures would give her away, but…nothing.

Now Zoe wasn't with him, the night air around him was horribly quiet. He started to get worried. Where on earth was—?

The next thing he knew, his head was under water and a four-limbed female limpet had clamped herself to his back, dragging him down, their combined body weight doing the job that she'd hadn't been able to achieve on her own.

He kicked hard and made some headway. She must have been holding her breath for quite some time, because suddenly she stopped fighting him and they both floated upwards.

When they broke the surface, she slid round to his side, hands locked behind his neck, ankles crossed over his opposite hip, and let him do the job of keeping them afloat. Once she'd gulped in enough air, she laughed triumphantly, letting the sound echo all the way to St Mawes.

And then there was silence again and they were staring at each other, bodies locked together, both breathing hard.

He shifted a little, brought her round so they were chest to chest, face to face. Her eyes widened and he felt her heart start to thump beneath the hand he had splayed on her ribcage.

She didn't say anything. No quick retort to make light of the situation, to ease awkwardness. She just looked back at him, breath held now, lips parted.

This time he didn't kiss Zoe St James because she pushed him to the end of his rope, or because an unwanted attraction had raged out of control. He didn't even have to kiss her to shut her up.

No, this time he kissed Zoe because he wanted to.

She was hesitant at first, letting him lead, but gradually she relaxed, softened and pulled him closer by sliding her arms around his neck. It was still there, the chemistry, crackling between them, even though he made sure this time was different, that he slowed things down so the kiss was soft and achingly light. He was surprised they hadn't lit the whole bay up with the sparks they must be generating.

Keeping both of them afloat got harder and harder, and eventually he had to break away. She instantly unhooked her legs, slid out of his arms and kicked away, going into retreat, but he caught her hand, tugged, as he started to propel himself towards the beach.

At first she resisted slightly, but no sound left her lips, no complaints arose, and then she swam with him, kicking with her legs and flapping with her free hand as he did. It wasn't long before he found sand beneath his toes and he dug his feet in to anchor himself. Zoe floated into him and he kissed her again as soon as she was close enough, and he enjoyed the fact that, because he was a good six inches taller than her, she couldn't reach the bottom and she had to cling on to him for support.

In fact, he decided he liked kissing Zoe St James very much. Not just because of the undeniable chemistry between them, but because, when she stopped talking and let all her barriers down like this, there was an intoxicating sweetness to her.

She kissed him slowly, almost innocently, savouring every sensation as if she couldn't quite believe it was happening and that he was part of a delicious dream she might wake from at any second. He defied any man not to be rendered helpless by a kiss like that.

She was a surprise, this one, that was for sure. A mix of intriguing contradictions. But hadn't she said 'new and unexpected' was good for the soul? And when she kissed a trail down his neck and tasted the salt on his collarbone, he decided she might have a point. He could easily get lost in this, forget about everything that had plagued him in the run-up to that torture of a wedding just a week ago.

Zoe's lips left his shoulder and she leaned in close to his ear. 'This isn't part of the plan, is it? Separate holidays, remember?' she whispered.

He moved his head so he could look at her. Her mouth was set in that familiar quirky smile, but her eyes were large and questioning. Vulnerable.

He ran the hand that had been pressed against her back, holding her to him, round to her waist, delighting in the soft curves. 'Do you *want* me to stop?' he whispered back.

She shuddered underneath his hands and, while her eyes grew even larger, she shook her head.

'I don't want separate holidays any more,' he said before kissing her just below her ear. 'That was a stupid plan.'

Her voice was breathy and barely audible when she answered. 'Then what do you want?'

'I want you.' He pulled her close again, dragged his lips across hers. 'I want a holiday with you.'

# CHAPTER TEN

DAMIEN lay awake on his bunk, staring into the darkness, hardly able to see anything in the cabin on this moonless night, even though the portholes weren't obscured. He checked his watch—three in the morning.

But he wasn't tossing and turning on the long berth in the main cabin, taking his frustration out on his pillow or tangling himself in his sleeping bag. He was perfectly calm and relaxed. In fact, he couldn't remember feeling this relaxed in a long time. He'd sunk straight into this serene state after the adrenalin rush brought on by kissing Zoe had worn off.

They'd eventually swum back to the boat, kissed some more, and then she'd said goodnight and retreated into her cabin, almost shyly. He got it. She was blindsided and a little scared. He supposed he should be too, but he couldn't seem to summon up the energy.

His gaze wandered over the interior of the cabin.

He was starting to be able to make out a shape here, a line there. *Dream Weaver* might not be the most state-of-the-art yacht on the high seas, but she was welcoming and comfortable and he'd really enjoyed sailing her for the last week. So much that he'd started to wonder if borrowing her for a couple of weekends a year was enough.

Zoe had a point. Perhaps he didn't have to wait for his dream yacht. Perhaps he *should* get a 'good enough for now' boat, one he could moor closer to London and sail when he liked.

Ah, Zoe…

She blew him away. But she wouldn't fit in his life long-term. Probably wouldn't want to, but maybe that was okay too. He'd spent—no, wasted—over a year pining for a woman who'd never be his. That was where his 'stick to the plan' mentality had got him. He'd got so fixated on the idea of Sara he hadn't been able to shake her loose from his head, even when he'd desperately wanted to.

Where had that plan got him romantically? Nowhere. So why had it taken him so long to work that out and decide to move on? It didn't make sense, even to himself.

But he had decided to put the past behind him

now, thankfully, and maybe this borrowed honeymoon had given him the perfect opportunity. He genuinely liked Zoe, and not just because of the strange, unexpected and rather explosive chemistry they seemed to have. She was good company, and she shook things up wherever she went.

Damien had an idea that maybe he *needed* a little shaking up, that maybe he'd got too entrenched in his ways in recent years, and he suspected his crewmate might just be good for him in that respect. In small doses.

So, while Zoe St James definitely *wasn't* the missing jigsaw piece in his future, maybe, if she was open to the idea, she could be his 'just for now' girl.

Oh, heck, thought Zoe, as she got dressed the following morning, sliding a sundress on over her swimming costume. But she was smiling, and she touched a fingertip to her bottom lip, then let the hand fall away again.

What are you doing? This is insanity.

You can't seriously be considering getting involved with this guy. He's too… And he's too… And you're definitely *not*.

Aw, phooey. He was hot. Seriously hot. And a

fabulous kisser. She might be mad *not* to follow this attraction wherever it may lead.

Wherever it did lead, one thing was sure: the end destination would never be an altar. And that was fine by Zoe. Thinking of Damien standing there, waiting for her, it gave her the heebie-jeebies. Too much like déjà vu. And she wasn't making that mistake again.

No, when she finally was ready to take that step she'd choose someone like her. Someone in her own league. Someone who wouldn't realise suddenly that he was punching *way* below his weight and do a flit. No. Lesson learned on that front.

But that didn't mean she couldn't have a little fun…

*Be careful*, a little voice in her head said as she opened her cabin door, pulse racing, a shoal of quicksilver fish darting around in her stomach. *Put some limits on it. Set some ground rules for yourself.*

*Have a plan.*

She opened her cabin door and went looking for Damien, still not quite sure how she was going to navigate the tricky line between fun and heartbreak. He was up already, his sleeping bag and pillow stowed away and the seating bench put back to normal, but there was no sign of him in the cabin. Her heart was thumping wildly now. She pulled in a breath and let it out slowly through pursed lips, and then she climbed the stairs into the cockpit.

Damien was leaning over the back of the boat, messing with the rope for the dinghy. He must have heard her coming because he turned round and gave her the most wonderful smile.

She felt herself blush furiously. What was up with that? She thought she'd given it up long ago, had decided one required a sense of shame to do such things. Even Damien had told her she had none.

'Hi,' she said, and found she had an almost irresistible urge to look down at her toes. She managed not to. Which was just as well because Damien's face crinkled even further.

'Hi.'

She felt all awkward. Didn't know what to do… Should she go and kiss him? Shake his hand? What?

Damien saved her from further dithering by crossing the space between them, wrapping his arms around her and kissing her soundly. Zoe didn't mind a bit. Top result as far as she was concerned. And it proved it hadn't been some elaborate dream brought on by dodgy pub grub—that a man like him could find a girl like her desirable.

But they couldn't stay like that all day, more's the pity, and eventually they came up for air, made some breakfast, got ready to set sail for the day.

It hovered in the air around them all day, though, as if there was some intoxicating chemical in the sunshine. She found herself smiling doing the most mundane things, and every time he caught her eye she thought her heart had stopped, but it always kicked back into life double strong, and then tap-danced for a few minutes inside her chest.

She'd forgotten what it was like, this heady sensation of being totally caught up in an attraction. For the last two years she'd avoided it. Not that she hadn't gone out, but she'd always seemed to pick men who were pleasant but not heart-stopping. She was so bored with *nice* now.

She'd forgotten what she'd been missing.

They didn't round the Lizard that day. Instead Damien took them upstream beyond Falmouth and St Mawes and they tacked up the River Fal, zigzagging from one bank to the other. After the rougher weather a couple of days earlier it was easy to work alongside each other. Comfortable. They were a good team.

When they dropped the sails and used the motor to explore one of the tidal creeks they discovered a gorgeous little medieval church on the bank, set incongruously in a garden of palm trees and tropical ferns. They dropped anchor close by and went ashore to explore the parish of St Just-in-Roseland.

Sitting on the grass in the church garden, looking out over the estuary bathed in bright golden light, Zoe turned to Damien.

'What are we doing?'

He lay back on the spiky grass and smiled at the sky. 'I think it's called relaxing, but I'm new to it. I'll let you know when I've got a handle on it.'

She poked him in the ribs, then lay down beside him. 'You know what I mean.'

He rolled over on to one side and looked at her. Zoe stared defiantly at the sky, watched a little turtle-shaped cloud chase a bigger, wispier one.

'What do you want it to be?' he asked softly, and the low rumble behind his words made it sound slightly naughty. She twisted her head round and gave him a penetrating look.

'Not games,' she said. 'Not pretending it's some-thing it's not. Let's be honest about it.'

'Agreed.' He nodded, a serious look creeping into his eyes. 'But does it need a label?'

She breathed out noisily. 'Maybe not. But I think it needs a time limit.'

He thought about that for a moment, chewed one side of his lip. She wasn't sure he'd liked what she'd said, but he saw the sense in it. 'Okay,' he said.

'We both know there's an obvious cut-off point.'

There. She'd saved him the trouble of saying it should end with the holiday.

He blinked and shrugged the shoulder that wasn't supporting him. 'That doesn't mean it doesn't mean anything,' he said gravely, those blue eyes boring into hers.

Thank you, she whispered inwardly. For being honest. For being brave. For not making me feel disposable.

'It means it's a summer fl—'

He pressed a finger to her lips. 'No labels, re-member? Let's just enjoy this for what it is, see where it leads us.'

She assumed a look of mock-seriousness and laid the back of her hand to his forehead. 'I'm sorry, but this is you—Damien Stone—saying these things. Are you sure you haven't got a temperature?'

He gently peeled her hand away from his head, turned her palm towards his mouth and did something amazing with his tongue that made Zoe's toes actually, truly curl up and her eyes slide closed. Whatever fever it was, it was catching.

She pushed hard against his chest with her free hand, sent him toppling backwards and, while he was still grunting in surprise, she swung one leg over and sat on top of him. Then she kissed him slowly, sensuously. *Hello*, the kiss said, *to whatever new thing this is*. It felt as if they'd crossed some invisible barrier into new territory and it needed to be marked somehow.

Damien didn't reach up for her or pull her to him. Instead he lay spreadeagled on the grass, a slight smile curving his lips as he kissed her back. 'To answer your first question,' he muttered between kisses, 'I don't know what this is.'

Zoe ran her hands up inside his T-shirt and let her fingers explore.

'But whatever it is,' he added hoarsely, 'it's certainly working for me.'

\* \* \*

Zoe felt like a goddess. There was something in-toxicating about being slap-bang in the centre of Damien Stone's attention. And while part of her panicked every time she noticed a similarity be-tween Damien and her ex, another part told it to just calm down please and take a breath.

She wasn't marrying this one, was she? It was safe. And they'd both been honest and upfront about their expectations. He wasn't going to leave her unexpectedly; they were going to leave each other at the end of the week. Mutual decision.

Six more days with Damien, with a man who made her heart skip because he enjoyed being with her. Six days when he'd look at her and she'd see fire ignite in his eyes. Six days to feel the comfort of his arms around her when she just needed to be close to someone.

It had been a long time since she'd let anyone close.

In fact, it had been a long time since she'd had that kind of physical contact with anyone—hugs that lasted more than a few seconds, a hand to hold, a warm body to mould herself against. The play-wrestling her brothers still attempted at fam-ily get-togethers didn't count. Really, it didn't.

With Damien it counted. And, while she knew

this couldn't last, she would be forever grateful to him for that. He was healing something inside her. Something she hadn't even known had been broken.

It was a blustery, sunny day and, rather than heading round Lizard Point and making progress to the Scillies, Damien had suggested sailing up the neighbouring Helford River to have lunch. Nothing fancy, just sandwiches and salad and a bottle of crisp white wine that had been chilling on the end of a rope over the side of the boat. She was sitting in the cockpit with Damien when he picked up the sketchbook she'd been doodling in before lunch.

'You're going to make these up when you get back,' he said, but there was no inflection at the end of the sentence. It wasn't really a question. He was like that. Driven, focused, specific. Things she'd previously despised about him that now made her shiver in anticipation. There was something to be said for a man who knew how to apply that attention to detail when it came to women. Oh, yes.

Zoe shrugged and took a sip of her wine. 'Probably.'

It was difficult. Those designs had somehow

become caught up in her head with the idea of having a shop, and she didn't know if she could make one real without the other. She'd have to wait, work on something else when she got back.

But Damien was learning to read her too well. 'Why not?' he asked.

Zoe gave him the kind of look that she knew used to make his red blood cells sizzle and pop, but nowadays it just caused him to do things like he did just then—carefully prise the wine glass from her fingers, place it on the bench, pull her on to his lap and kiss her.

She was so dizzy when he'd finished with her that she told him about her dream for a workshop, for getting clients who would commission one-of-a-kind pieces with her unique twist to them. A chance to really let her imagination fly.

'So…look for properties when you get back,' he said. 'Start small, build up.'

She shook her head. 'I'm not ready for that yet. I'm not at that stage. It's still early days.'

'What do you need to get it to that stage, then?'

Zoe picked up her wine glass again and pressed it to her chest, the fingers of both hands wrapped around the stem. 'I need to visit the bank manager, make some kind of projections, I suppose...'

Get some guts.

Damien used a finger to tip her chin up and make her look at him.

'You can do this,' he said seriously. 'You've got spark, you've got flair. You can make this happen, even if you're not so good with the organising side of things. Doesn't matter. Get an assistant who is.'

Zoe stuttered, although she wasn't sure which word was stalling on her tongue.

'It'd be a shame to never see these designs made up,' he said. 'So do it.'

'I...I can't.'

Where had that come from? She hadn't been planning on saying that at all.

Damien, as always, zeroed in on the root of the problem, but there was such a tenderness in his eyes that she found herself saying more things she hadn't planned.

'I'm scared.'

His thumb stroked her chin. 'Of what?'

Zoe didn't know. She was just scared. Scared of trying and failing, maybe. Of investing in something with all her heart only to see it wither and die.

She pulled her chin away from his hand and

looked down. 'I wouldn't expect you to understand this, but not everybody's dreams come true. Not everyone can do what you do.'

Much to her surprise, Damien began to laugh. But the warm, rich sound she was used to was now dark and self-mocking. 'You think I get everything I want out of life?' He ran a hand through his hair and looked away momentarily. 'Believe me, I don't.'

She clutched the stem of her glass even harder. 'What dreams are still eluding you? I can't believe you've got much left on your to-do list! You're successful and confident and clever.'

His eyes flashed with sudden warmth and she knew he was grateful for the compliments, which struck her as odd because surely he knew all these things about himself.

'What am I known for, Zoe? What do people joke about me?'

Well, she knew what *she* used to say about him, but now was really not a good time to re-hash that, so she thought harder. 'That you're always the best man, I suppose. But even that's not fair. A man just looks better and better the more times he gets asked to do that. Me, I've only been a bridesmaid once and I've already got my mother telling me

I'd better not make a habit of it, especially since I've got one false start under my belt.'

He squeezed her hand and his expression became more sombre. 'I understand, because I feel the same way. Don't you think I'd like to be the groom instead of the best man some day?'

Now it was Zoe's turn to laugh. 'Well, I don't think you're going to have any trouble on that score. I mean, look at you! They must be queuing up around the block.'

Damien didn't join her. There wasn't one glint of amusement in those hard blue eyes. Zoe exhaled and looked deep into her wine glass. 'If you want it so much, why haven't you got married before now?'

She felt him go still underneath her. This conversation had got too serious to be sitting on his lap, but she didn't know how to get off without making it seem like a judgement of some kind. And she of all people knew just how much it hurt to be judged when you were down.

'Haven't found the right girl?' she asked softly, trying to inject a bit of levity into this rapidly sinking conversation.

When he didn't reply she looked up at him.

'Something like that,' he said wearily.

And then a sudden knowledge hit Zoe. Where it had come from she didn't know, but she realised she and Damien had more in common than she'd thought. 'You liked someone and they didn't like you back the same way.'

Like her and Aiden. She'd worshipped him, but she suspected she'd just been an amusing diversion for him. Some mad impulse he'd thought better of eventually.

Damien's hands came around her waist and he lifted her off him and stood up. The non-slip bench was rough and cold against her legs. He sighed and walked over to the back of the boat, staring out at the water below. 'Pretty much. She was in love with someone else.'

Zoe put her wine glass down again and went to him, curled her arms around his body and pressed herself against his back.

'It'll happen for you,' she said. 'I know it.'

'How do you know?' he replied, and his tone held a tinge of bleakness.

She tugged on his T-shirt, pulled him round to face her and looked up into his face. He placed his hands on her shoulders and looked searchingly into her eyes, as if he was trying to read what she was going to say before her lips moved.

'Because you're a leading man,' she said. 'You're that type that good things happen to.'

Confusion clouded his features. 'What?'

He hadn't been expecting her to say that, had he? Now she needed to explain.

'It's like in the movies,' she began, and Damien's expression became sceptical. She slapped him on the chest. 'Hear me out, at least.'

One corner of his mouth twitched, so Zoe continued.

'I have a theory that there are two types of people in this world—the romantic leads and the backup characters. Romantic leads are the sort of people we'd all like to be, or be with, like—' she stopped herself saying *you*, thinking he'd scoff and stop listening '—like Sara.'

There was a flicker of something on his face. 'Go on.'

Zoe shrugged and smiled. 'I have to tell you that it's hard work being best friends with a girl like her. She's pretty, clever, sweet... Good things come her way naturally. She hardly has to even try. Look at her now, off in Paradise with the man of her dreams. I mean, you can't get any jammier than that, can you?'

Damien pursed his lips. He was listening to her intently now.

'And what about the other sort?'

'Oh, the sidekicks? They get their happy endings too…sometimes. It's just that it's not always as shiny and perfect. Some of them have to compromise, settle a little.'

'The two don't mix?'

She shook her head emphatically. 'Well, not long-term. The honourable best friend might date the girl for a bit, and we all think he's adorable, but you know she's going to end up with the leading man.'

Damien frowned. 'Is that what you're trying to tell me? That I need to set my sights lower?'

Zoe's mouth dropped open. He really thought that was what she meant? She gave him a shove with the flat of her hand, then, before he lost balance, she clutched on to the front of his T-shirt and pulled him down towards her for a kiss.

'No, you daft man,' she whispered. 'I'm saying you're the other sort. Look at your life, all you've accomplished. The rest will come too. Just don't lose hope.'

Damien slid his hands down to her waist and pulled her even closer, began to kiss the soft patch of skin between jaw and ear. 'So, if I'm a leading man, who are you?'

Zoe let her head drop back to give him better access. She blocked out the pang of sorrow that spiked through her at his words. Not the same, she whispered silently to herself. But she had other words to say out loud.

'I'm the girl who's making the most of having him wrapped around her, that's who.'

# CHAPTER ELEVEN

Down a cobbled street in Falmouth was a second-hand bookshop stuffed to the brim with both yellowing volumes with a few decades' worth of dust on them and dog-eared bestsellers from last Christmas. Damien discovered it had quite a good sailing section, not surprising, he supposed, for a shop in a town like this, where white sails decorated the waterfront on almost every day of the year.

He'd moored here plenty of times before when he'd been with Luke, but he'd never been to this curious little shop, never mind this street, always in too much of a hurry to re-stock and sail on.

There'd been plenty of other places on the large and sprawling estuary that he'd never visited either, but Zoe seemed to have a talent for sniffing these things out, and he was rather enjoying staying put, using Falmouth as a base and discovering the things that he'd never noticed before. Reaching the Scillies was now looking less and less probable, but somehow he didn't mind.

Zoe squealed. 'I don't believe it!'

She came running through labyrinthine bookshelves towards him, clutching a large coffee-table book, and almost sent half a display flying in her enthusiasm to reach him. He smiled. Once he'd thought her 'too much', but now he found her verve a little bewitching. Things were certainly never dull when Zoe was around.

'Look!' she said, almost yelling, and shoved the book so close to his face he couldn't focus on it.

He took hold of it and moved it to a distance where he wasn't required to go cross-eyed. 'Beautiful Beaches of Britain.'

She tugged it away from his grasp and started to leaf through it, cooing and making all sorts of exclamatory noises. That was Zoe. She couldn't just say *Oh!;* she had a whole rainbow of responses.

She had a whole rainbow of responses to him too. Sometimes she was bold and bossy, sometimes she was soft and almost shy. He never knew what he was going to get from one moment to the next. It was a bit like a roller coaster, with all of the thrills and adrenalin. Perhaps it was just as well this wasn't going to be a long-term thing.

He'd like to enjoy his time with Zoe, not reach a point where he was numb and slightly nauseous and wanted nothing more than to leave it behind.

She smiled up at him. 'My aunt had this book. I used to flick through it every time we visited. I dreamed of visiting each and every one of these beaches, especially the dramatic cliff-backed ones in Devon and Cornwall. Look at that—!'

She thrust the book at him. He had to admit, it was a very fine picture of Kynace Cove, with its dramatic rocky shore and island reached by a bar of sand at low tide, not too far away from where they were now.

'So which ones do you still have to cross off your list?'

Zoe stopped smiling and her mouth hung slightly open. 'Um…'

He waited for her to remember the names, or at least point to a picture in the book. It was at least a minute before he realised that answer would never come.

'You haven't been to any of them yet, have you?'

She shook her head.

Damien chuckled in bemusement. 'Why not? You're all grown up now. You've got a car and a free weekend every now and then. What's stopped you?'

Zoe closed the book softly and tucked it under her arm. 'Nothing, I suppose. But I...'

Damien tipped his head to one side, a lopsided smile on his face. Zoe moved the book to her front and crossed her arms over it. She looked a little confused.

'I just liked looking at the pictures...' She trailed off, obviously reliving some long-archived memory. 'These beaches seemed like dreams, not real places I could actually go to one day.' She frowned. 'That's stupid, isn't it?'

'What would be stupid would be not taking the opportunity to visit some of them when we're so close.'

The expression on Zoe's face almost made him laugh again, but he held it in. Even though they'd been sailing round the Devon and Cornwall coast for over a week now, she hadn't thought to mention this before? The possibility must have crossed her mind.

'You think we really could?' she said a little breathlessly.

Damien pulled her close, book and all, and pressed a kiss to the tip of her nose. 'We made a deal—I'm your deck hand and skipper for the next five days. I'll take you anywhere you want to go.'

Zoe's response was so enthusiastic that she dropped the book on Damien's toe.

Zoe ran up to the front of the boat as they neared Polkerris Beach. She hung on to the metal rails of the parapet and leaned forward, Titanic-style, her arms outstretched.

The photo in her aunt's book had only paid partial tribute to its beauty. Steep, rock-scarred hills rose either side of a swirl of pale yellow beach, held safe from the changeable Cornish weather by the protective arm of a curved sea wall at one end. She knew this beach had inspired a famous novelist, and Zoe had liked that book of hers when she'd read it at school, the one about the girl trying to fill another woman's shoes and not really succeeding. She'd have to read it again when she got home.

She turned to grin at Damien back in the cockpit. They'd abandoned the idea of the Scilly Isles and opted to stay in the Falmouth area, as it was the perfect base for exploring the wonderful local beaches. This was the third one she could tick off her list, the third of her childhood wishes granted. And this man had made them happen.

That night after they'd been to the bookshop he'd settled down at the navigation table on *Dream Weaver* and had got out his maps and charts. Zoe had tried to join him, but the little bench seat had clearly been made for one and she didn't have the right kind of skinny behind to slide in beside him, so she'd hugged him from behind, hanging round his neck like a college boy's sweater, until he'd shooed her away.

She hadn't even minded that he'd been completely absorbed for the next hour or so, or that she'd fallen asleep on the long cabin bench Damien used as a berth reading her book. She'd woken later in the night to find herself covered with an opened-out sleeping bag, his unconscious form across from her on the opposite bench.

Damien might have ignored her, but she hadn't cared because no one had ever done anything to make her feel so special.

Oh, she knew that had been the deal they'd made on that first morning—that he'd take her where she wanted to go. But a lot had changed since then. It wasn't because he had to any more, but because he'd wanted to.

Plans had changed. She had changed. She'd even go so far as to say that Damien had undergone a transformation, but she wasn't really sure that was true. She'd just tarred him with Aiden's brush from the beginning, not seen what was right in front of her.

He wasn't anything like Aiden. Not really.

Yes, he had the same ilk of good looks, the same kind of confidence, but Damien was kind and thoughtful where her ex had been self-important and shallow. She shuddered to think back to how much she'd adored him now, how much she'd let herself disappear and change to please him. But it had never been enough.

She should have seen the warning signs; they'd been there, after all.

She should have minded that he used to joke about their initials to friends constantly, as if he'd come up with the funniest gag in the world and couldn't resist sharing it. 'I'm the A and she's the Z,' he used to say, and Zoe had laughed along, even though, after the fourth airing, her smile had become pinched instead of open.

She turned her attention back to the sunny beach. She didn't want to think about Aiden any more. And Damien never made her feel like that—second class to his first class.

A pair of strong, warm arms closed around her. A taut, muscled body pressed against her back. Zoe stayed with her arms outstretched, eyes closed, and breathed in the moment. Pretty soon a pair of soft, firm lips began to work their way up from her collarbone to her ear. She twisted as he got there to kiss him properly, even though it made her neck ache horribly.

'I've got to drop the anchor or we'll float all the way to Portugal,' he mumbled against her lips.

Zoe sighed. 'If you have to.'

He gave her a nudge. 'You're in my way,' he whispered in her ear, his low voice tickling her skin and making her break out into goosebumps.

'Give me a minute. I just need to finish my *moment*.'

Damien just rumbled a laugh as she faced front and began to sing.

'What *are* you doing? Calling whales?'

She reached behind and slapped him wherever she could reach. 'It's the song from the film. Join in! You might as well. We've got you, me, the front of a boat…It's the least we can do to provide the soundtrack.' And she carried on singing into the wind.

Damien just laughed harder, picked her up in his arms and threw her into the vibrant blue water. When Zoe came to the surface, spluttering a little and wiping the curls from her eyes, she yelled, 'What was that for?' But she didn't mind, not really. Damien was surprising her, doing things she'd never thought he'd do, and it was turning her carefully constructed walls into chocolate.

He was busy letting the chain out to drop the anchor. 'I fast-forwarded. That's how the film ends, after all.'

She paddled her legs to keep herself afloat. 'I think you'll find the hero ends up in a much more sorry state than you are. Still…there's time yet!'

Damien finished his job and stood smiling down at her, hands on hips, legs apart. Zoe couldn't help smiling back.

It was working. She was letting go of all that baggage she'd been dragging around with her since the night of her hen do, and it was such a relief to see it float away and disappear. She couldn't remember a time when she'd been happier.

And then there was a splash and Zoe's eyes were

sprayed with salt water. She opened them again to find him swimming towards her. Her heart kicked and the resulting adrenalin spike made her want to move, to run. To fly. Since she could do neither of those things, she settled for swimming.

'Last one to the beach is a rotten egg,' she shouted, then set off to churn up the waves with her notoriously haphazard front crawl. Damien would probably catch her, but Zoe decided she didn't mind that one bit.

That night they moored where they had the first night they'd arrived in the Fal estuary: opposite the little beach with the stone cottage. But time had moved on and a few days had turned the previously absent moon into a sliver of pale shimmering white just above the horizon. When they jumped in the water the magic was gone.

It doesn't last, Zoe reminded herself. Magic like this doesn't last.

And neither would her time with Damien; she needed to remember that. Only…sometimes it was so difficult. She knew this was dangerous, knew it would be so easy to tumble head over heels for this man.

Only a few more days together. The tide on their

holiday had turned and now they were heading in a different direction. Tomorrow they were setting sail back off up the coast towards the River Dart and Lower Hadwell. And then they'd go their separate ways and it would all be a beautiful memory. As long as she could last out, hold onto her heart for a few more days, she'd be okay. She could last that long, couldn't she?

Easier said than done in a setting like this, she thought, as she peeled her T-shirt off over her swimming costume. She didn't even think twice about it now, even though she got uncharacteristically shy normally when displaying her curves, but Damien seemed to like them, and suddenly it didn't seem quite as important to keep the flimsy cotton barrier on.

This time she followed Damien's lead and jumped straight in. He was right. It was easier that way, rather than prolonging the torture by climbing in slowly.

They swam to the beach and strolled along it, holding hands, stopping every now and then to wind themselves round each other and kiss. The beach was even more beautiful with a touch of moonlight to turn its sand bluish-white.

Damien stopped walking and pulled her to him,

his hands exploring her bare torso, his lips working the magic that the water had forgotten.

She knew where this was leading and twin
desires warred inside her—the desire to have
Damien completely, to know him completely, and
the desire to keep herself safe. It had taken two
years to get over Aiden's betrayal and, while she
knew Damien wasn't like that, it wouldn't do to
fall for him. This wasn't to have and to hold, to
love and to cherish; it was just for now.

Just a few more days. People did this all the
time—had flings, walked away unscathed. So
could she. And being with Damien would be...
amazing. So what if she hadn't quite managed to
sleep with anyone else since Aiden? She'd moved
on. She was ready now.

He pulled away and she could tell he was looking at her intently just by the way he brushed his
thumb across her cheek. 'I'd really like to take
you out to dinner when we get back to London,'
he said.

That was when Zoe began to wobble. Inside.
*Say no.*

A fling with a time limit was one thing.
Something they took home, carried on back in
London? That was too much like a relationship

for Zoe's liking. She'd never be able to hold herself back emotionally, not if it went on for weeks or, heaven help her, months. She couldn't fall for him. Not this one. Another man who wouldn't want her for ever.

At least this one had the honesty to say that up-front, though.

She pulled away, tried to wriggle out of his grasp. 'I'll race you back to the boat,' she said brightly and stepped back.

Damien caught her hand. Gently. Far too gently. Zoe felt moisture well behind her eyes for some reason. *Please let me go*, she begged silently. *I need some distance, some kind of barrier.*

He didn't pull her back to him, but stepped towards her, keeping his grip round her wrist feather-light. She was glad it was too dark to see the look in his eyes. That might have been her undoing.

'What's wrong?' he said gently, and his free hand reached out to touch her face.

Zoe closed her eyes, partly to block him out, partly to stop the bead of moisture hanging on her lashes from falling onto his fingers and giving herself away. She shook her head, effectively dislodging his hand and refuting his words in one small motion.

He moved closer, but he didn't touch her again. He even let go of her wrist. 'I know you,' he said, his voice low and far too soft. 'Don't hide from me.'

*But I need to. I really do.*

It was happening already, wasn't it? She could feel herself melting under his touch, her chest squeezing painfully from his tenderness and concern for her. Even with the stupid time limit, she wasn't safe. She should have realised. She shouldn't do what she'd been planning to do with him now. It would seal her fate.

He kissed her softly, tenderly, almost drawing her secrets from her. Zoe's throat tightened even as her lips moved in tandem with his. She couldn't hold back, not any longer. So she threw away all her masks, let down every last barrier and kissed him the way she'd always wanted to, telling him what she would never say with her lips.

That was when things got really scary. And wonderful.

They were doing more than just kissing now. They were communicating. And, while their bodies were still—just about—clothed, it felt as if whoever Damien and Zoe were inside those cases of flesh and bones and nerves were totally naked. Transparent. Zoe found she couldn't breathe. She'd never realised it could be this way, but it was too… It was too much.

She pulled her lips from his, pushed her hands on his chest to help her gather just a few inches of distance before she lost herself completely.

Her voice was hoarse and thready when she spoke. 'I know we said this was a fling,' she began. 'But I don't know if I'm ready to…'

She didn't say the last bit. Coward.

Damien's warm arms closed around her shoulders, pulled her close. She laid her cheek against his chest and breathed him in.

'If there's one thing I've learned this week, it's that rushing to the destination sometimes robs the journey of its joy,' he said softly.

A wave of something washed over Zoe. She called it gratitude, but she feared it was something else.

'I know it will be amazing,' Damien said softly as his fingers ran lightly down her back, making her shiver, 'but it has to feel right for both of us.'

Zoe really wanted to tell him she wasn't sure that was such a good idea, but the soft seductive tone of his voice and the lazy circles of his fingers on the back of her hips had severed the connection between brain and tongue.

'So let's not end it now. I've spent too much of my life sticking doggedly to a self-imposed timetable. I want to do things the way you do it. I want to savour the experience, enjoy the journey, not miss the best bits because I'm rushing to the end goal.'

She shivered again, but it was nothing to do with his fingers and everything about the thought of Damien applying his new philosophy to his lovemaking. That approach could make a girl very, *very* happy.

His voice was low and coaxing in her ear. 'So, have dinner with me on Saturday night, Zoe, when we get back. Let's see where this thing can go.'

Unfortunately, while her head was firing excuse after excuse in his direction, her mouth just said, very clearly and politely, 'I'd like that.'

Oh, you stupid girl. You shouldn't have said that.

But the warm ball of hope that had ignited inside her chest at his words had completely derailed all her good intentions.

Maybe there was a chance. Maybe he really, really liked her.

And, for now, *maybe* was enough because Zoe St James had not just discovered she could dream again, but she was learning how to tug their delicate strings and pull those far-off images towards reality.

They'd been lucky with the weather, they knew that, but their luck didn't hold much longer. The forecast two days later wasn't terrible; it just wasn't that good either. Damien loved it, of course. Scudding clouds and an impatient breeze behind *Dream Weaver*. Zoe, not so much, but he kept her busy on deck, where she wasn't as fond of the pitch of the boat as he was—she was still only just discovering her sea legs—but she was learning the basics well. If she ever decided to keep this up, she could be a pretty decent sailor. She had the instinct for it.

They headed for Bantham Beach anyway, but when they dropped the sail and surveyed the shore Damien held off lowering the anchor. Zoe came to join him in the cockpit and stared landward with him. 'Problem?'

Damien nodded. 'The water is shallow here quite a way out, and the surf is pounding against that shore. The flags say swimming would be dangerous, and the dinghy would probably flip over.'

'So it's no go for this one.'

'Not from a seaward approach, anyway.' He made rueful face. 'Sorry.'

Zoe frowned and stared at the beach. He waited for her to say something funny and biting to take the edge off her disappointment, but she just closed her mouth and put her hands on her hips.

She'd been in a strange mood all day yesterday: one moment enthusiastic and funny as always, the next quiet and pensive. Distant. As if she was backing away from him, which didn't make sense. He'd have thought she'd be pleased he wanted to see her again after their holiday. Maybe she didn't like him as much as he thought.

And that would be a pity. He discovered he could relax around her. Probably because, since they hadn't exactly warmed to each other on first meeting, he'd never gone into full-out *impress* mode. And it was a little late to start now. Zoe had already seen more of his bad side than most people did. However, it hadn't put her off completely, and it was kind of refreshing not to have to live up to his own reputation.

She turned away from the beach and sighed. 'It

doesn't look as pretty as the picture in the book, anyway.'

He took a long, hard look at the shore, the jagged grey rocks piercing the flat and endless sand, the dunes behind them covered in fluffy grass. On a sunny summer's day this would be the perfect place for a family: rock pools aplenty to explore, a wide beach that shelved gently, leaving plenty of warm places where the sun heated shallow pools of sea water when the tide went out. But now the tide was in, angry and grey, and the breakers over the shallow sand relentless.

'A different kind of pretty, maybe. But the beach hasn't changed, has it? Just the weather. Maybe it's all in the way you look at it?'

She sat down on the cockpit bench. He sensed she couldn't quite bear to look at the source of disappointment. He could understand that, he supposed. This had been one of her favourites.

'We could always try again tomorrow,' he said.

'We've got to have this boat back on its mooring in two days, you said. I thought the schedule was pretty tight.'

It was. But he wanted to do this for her, see her happy again. 'We'll see.'

Zoe's arms dropped and hung limp by her side.

'Maybe this one wasn't supposed to come true.' And then she stood up and loped down the stairs into the cabin.

He wanted to go to her, kiss her until he saw that naughty sparkle in her eyes again, but the weather wouldn't allow it. They were too close to the shore and he couldn't let *Dream Weaver* drift in this kind of weather. It would have to wait until they reached dry land.

For some reason, he started thinking about what she'd told him the first night they'd moored at the beach, about her fiancé. His mind had drifted in that direction quite a few times in the last few days.

What must it have been like? To have the whole of your life mapped out, a date set, a venue booked, dress chosen and fitted...for it all to come to nothing? He understood now why she had that cynical streak, why, despite her exuberant positive personality, she was reluctant to hope and plan for even little things. It wasn't a weakness of character that prevented her from pursuing her dreams, just the scars of previous failed attempts. And Damien knew himself just how hard those things could sting.

She came back out on deck an hour later, helped

him as they prepared to sail into Salcombe for the night. Her smile was back on, her wit at one hundred per cent capacity. He knew it for what it was now. Emotional wallpaper. And so thin. How had he ever thought her hard and insensitive?

It made him want to turn the boat round, sail back to that beach and command the sun to come out, the waves to be still. However, despite the cracks that some of his friends made, even he didn't have the power to do those things, so he stayed silent and guided the boat up the river and towards the busy marina.

But it bothered him that he couldn't. He wanted to do something to thank her for all she'd done for him. This holiday had been just what he needed and he was ready to face life back at home now.

*Then why aren't you ready to say goodbye, if you're ready to move on?*

So he wasn't ready to end whatever he had with Zoe yet. That didn't mean anything. He and Zoe were combustible chemicals. Great for an instant reaction, but long-term they would be destructive. She wasn't right for his life, nor he for hers. Okay, that mental jigsaw picture of his future did not have a Zoe-shaped hole in the middle, but he was having fun. What was so wrong with that?

When they reached the marina he jumped off *Dream Weaver* to secure the bowline and as he did so he realised something.

He didn't think that hole was Sara-shaped either now. He could see someone *like* her in the picture if he tried, and that was progress, wasn't it? Zoe had distracted him enough to help him get his bearings, to at least start the process, and he was very grateful to her for that.

So why wasn't he happier? Why did he feel as if he'd been using her somehow, even if they'd both come into this with their eyes open and on equal terms?

## CHAPTER TWELVE

THE last beach on the list Damien had drawn up for Zoe was Blackpool Sands, only a short distance from the Dart estuary, and they had just enough time to visit it before they left the open sea and headed upriver to Lower Hadwell for their last night aboard *Dream Weaver*.

There had been six beaches they'd wanted to visit, and they'd managed them all—bar one. Maybe one day, Zoe thought.

She knew she ought to do what Damien had suggested: make plans, book a free weekend in her calendar and drive down to add that extra tick to her list. There were still a few weeks before the weather would get colder and the leaves started to turn.

Next summer, maybe. Or the one after that.

Not yet. Because the thought of returning on her own was making her feel strangely depressed. And, really, it was time to concentrate on her career now. She didn't have the time or money to

gallivant around the country if she really wanted
to get a shop up and running.

She watched Damien drag the dinghy from
where it had been lashed to the deck and throw
it overboard, keeping hold of the painter. How
different he seemed from the night of Sara and
Luke's wedding. He moved easily, fluidly, the
muscles across his back shifting under his T-shirt.
It hardly seemed the same body she'd done a tense
rumba with almost a fortnight ago.

In fact, now that she knew him better, she realised he'd been unusually tense that night. Hadn't
he said as much when he'd apologised for kissing her? At the time she'd thought it was a lousy
excuse, but maybe there'd been some truth to it.

The dinghy was in the water now and Damien
was walking it round to the ladder at the stern,
dragging it by its yellow rope.

Weddings were always stressful, she supposed.
Especially if you'd been as close to the centre of
the action as she and Damien had been.

No, that didn't sit right. The Damien she knew
was contained and focused under pressure.
Something had been different. He must have been
*really* stressed. She knew now she'd never have
been able to push him over the edge the way she

had otherwise. If she didn't know how happy he'd been for Luke and Sara, she'd have thought the whole idea of them getting married bothered him somehow.

The dinghy was ready now and he grinned at her. She smiled back.

Oh, well. Whatever it had been, he was all better now and that was what counted, wasn't it?

While not as Mediterranean-like as the weather they'd been blessed with the previous week, it was a passably pleasant day. The sun could occasionally be spotted between the slow-drifting clouds and the temperature was mild. It certainly hadn't stopped the holidaymakers flocking to this popular beach, even though it was a mile or two from the nearest town.

They left *Dream Weaver* anchored in the deeply shelving bay and took the dinghy the short distance to the shore. Jagged pink-tinged cliffs rose either side of the beach, topped with bright green tufty grass and populated by unimpressed sheep. A crescent of perfect golden shingle—fine enough to look like sand, but not fine enough to walk on without hopping now and then—arced gracefully between cliffs and road and deep blue water.

The proximity of the road meant that, unlike

many of the beaches they'd visited that week, it had a car park and toilets, a café and a surf shop. After the relative seclusion of some of those other beaches, this one was all noise and colour and movement. It felt like a return to civilisation, the real world, and Zoe wasn't sure she liked that that much. The real world was close enough as it was. Let her have the last day of her fantasy holiday without being reminded it was almost over.

However, as they hopped out of the dinghy and pulled out of reach of the crashing surf, she and Damien felt like a unit of two. She hung on to that feeling.

It wouldn't be the same when they got back home, would it? Damien might change his mind about that dinner in the cold, grey light of a London morning. And maybe that would be a blessing in disguise. There would be plenty of other women around, most of them more glamorous than she was. On the boat, with just the two of them, it had been fine, but Zoe didn't do well with comparisons. She was never the first one a man's eyes went to when she went out with her single friends. Especially if that friend had been Sara.

Once the dinghy was safe they headed for the

café. Zoe sat on one of the weathered picnic tables while Damien went to get ice cream. He returned with a cardboard holder containing six cones, all in different colours and flavours, and plonked them down in front of her while he started on his own plain vanilla.

Zoe laughed nervously. 'What's all this? You can't possibly want to fatten me up.'

Damien's mouth kept smiling but his eyes told her he wasn't happy with her comment. Nothing he hadn't told her in person over the last few days, nothing his obvious attraction for her hadn't chipped away at. But making a joke about her size was a hard habit to break. How else was she supposed to stop someone jumping in and doing it first? At least this way she controlled the damage, didn't look like a pity case.

She flashed a look back that communicated both exasperation and contrition. His eyes regained their sparkle.

'I got one of each flavour for you so could try them all, pick which one you like, and leave me to eat mine in peace.' And he took a huge lick of his ice cream, as if to demonstrate.

Zoe left the cones to drip while she extracted herself from her side of the picnic bench and went to sit on Damien's lap. He held his cone at arm's length, just in case, and Zoe hit him lightly on the chest. But hitting turned to touching and then she kissed him, slowly and sweetly enough not to shock any onlookers, but thoroughly enough to accomplish her goal and sweep her tongue along his lips and then inside his mouth.

She pulled back. 'Vanilla's not bad.'

Damien sat there looking a little stunned. 'If that's what buying more than one cone gets me, I'm going to do it more often,' he said gruffly.

Zoe just laughed. *More often.* He hadn't changed his mind yet, then. And she was going to make the most of that.

Right then she decided that tonight she should grab whatever bliss was on offer, make the most of a gorgeous man and a secluded boat. She'd deal with the fallout when they got back home. She knew it was reckless, but she couldn't walk away without greedily taking what she could. She wouldn't live her life wondering what it would have been like. Aiden had taught her she couldn't plan for success in matters of the heart, but that didn't mean she had to plan for failure instead, did it?

She pulled the cardboard holder over, selected

the vanilla and started to lick. She didn't even slurp each of the others to see what she was missing. In fact, she donated them to a family passing by with some incredibly whiney children. The mother gave her a grateful look. Well, she did before her gaze moved to Damien and the woman almost walked into a pole.

Zoe's choice of flavour, and she was sticking to it.

Her choice.

Maybe that was where the answer lay? Instead of waiting for someone to relegate her to second choice, maybe she should be the one making the decisions for once. And the way she felt right now, with Damien's arms around her waist, the memory of warm vanilla from his lips mixing with the cold, fresh stuff from her cone, she wondered if she dared choose *this* man—the one who had pushed her over the last edge of her resistance by buying her a tray of multicoloured ice creams.

*Dream Weaver* rounded a bend in the river and Zoe watched the pastel coloured houses of Lower Hadwell appear with a sense of heaviness inside. Tonight they'd take the yacht back to her mooring, tidy her up and leave her ready for Luke and Sara's next visit.

After lunch tomorrow they'd both be away. Separate cars. She hoped it wouldn't be separate lives.

Was it wrong to hope for more? Because hope she did, even though she knew she wasn't Damien's usual type, knew that there would be more than a few raised eyebrows among their mutual friends when it became common knowledge that something was going on between them.

They secured *Dream Weaver* at the little marina and went below decks to start packing and tidying, after which they planned to have a leisurely dinner at The Ferryman. While she tidied, Zoe was making good use of her imagination to form *other* plans she had for Damien that night.

She had her head in the cupboard opposite the bathroom, replacing Luke's oilskin, when a muffled tinny tune chimed out from inside her cabin.

Her mobile phone!

The coverage had been so patchy for the last couple of weeks she'd almost forgotten she owned it. She quickly extricated her head and shoulders from the cupboard and launched herself into her cabin, throwing the top half of her body on to the bunk and grabbing at the little shelf on the wall where she'd left her handset.

It stopped ringing just as her fingers closed around it. She wiggled herself back off the bunk, stood up and inspected the screen.

Sara?

Why on earth was she phoning from the Caribbean? It would cost a fortune.

Zoe wandered into the main cabin, phone in hand, looking bemused. Damien looked up. 'Problem?'

She frowned. 'Don't know. I missed a call from Sara. I don't know why she—'

The phone leapt to life in her hand and she quickly pressed the button and answered. 'Hi, darling! What are you doing calling me from Paradise?'

There was a loud sniff on the other end of the line, and when Sara spoke her voice was tight and strained. 'I'm not in Paradise. I'm at Heathrow.'

Zoe dropped the phone but, luckily, she caught it with her other hand. Damien took a step closer as she pressed it back to her ear.

'You're at the airport? But you're not supposed to be back until the day after tomorrow!'

'I know,' Sara wailed. 'It's over, Zoe. The whole thing is messed up!'

Zoe's stomach went cold. 'What's over?'

'Me and Luke.'

Time stopped. Zoe's mouth refused to do anything but hang open uselessly. She swallowed and forced her vocal cords to work. 'So where's Luke?' she asked hoarsely. She was afraid she knew the answer that was coming and she didn't think she was going to like it.

Another bubbly sniff. 'Antigua, I think.'

There it was. Zoe met Damien's concerned gaze.

'You came home on your own?' she asked quietly.

Damien was closer now, his eyes fixed on her phone.

She didn't know what to do. This wasn't Sara—dramatic departures and drama queen moments. Those sorts of things were Zoe's department. Think, she told herself. What would Sara do? How would she calm you down if you were the one having the meltdown? Be like Sara—you always wanted to be and this is your chance.

Even better, she thought with a flash of inspiration, be like *Damien*. He always knew how to handle sticky situations. She'd think ahead, not just react.

'Zoe?'

'I'm here,' she said softly.

'I can't go home, Zo. Luke and I had a horrible fight. We've never had an argument like that before and I can't go back to a house full of wedding gifts waiting to be opened. I don't know what to do.'

Sara's volume was rising along with her pitch. Zoe could tell she was close to losing it completely.

'You stay right where you are,' she said. 'Book yourself into one of the airport hotels, text me the details and I'll be there as soon as I can.'

Sara sniffed. 'Okay.'

'Just don't do anything—' Zoe managed to stop herself saying *else* '—stupid, okay?'

'Okay.' She heard Sara pull in a steadying breath.

'Take a bath, order some room service and I'll see you soon.' After a few more reassuring comments Zoe rang off.

Damien's expression was taut when she looked up. He spoke quickly, words tripping over themselves to get out of his mouth. 'How is she? What happened?'

He had that look again, that look of a caged animal he'd had just before he'd given his speech at the wedding reception.

Zoe shook her head and stared back down at her phone. 'I don't know.' She met his eyes. 'They had a fight and she flew home. She's very upset.'

Damien paced down the cabin away from her and back again. Then he grabbed his jacket and started hunting for some keys. Car keys.

'What are you doing?' Zoe asked, her jaw tight.

'I was going to…' He looked up, slightly dazed, and shook his head. 'I don't know. I wanted to help.'

A hundred little details about Damien, about Luke, about Sara, came flooding into Zoe's head. First and foremost were mental snapshots of the wedding, images Zoe hadn't even realised her memory had stored: how tense Damien had seemed before the service had started, the way he'd stared at Sara when she'd walked down the aisle. The way he'd dried up just before his speech and the look on his face when he'd stared over her shoulder when they'd been dancing together.

None of those things meant anything on their

own, but seen rapidly together as a montage of memories...

And then his words about the mystery girl in his past came floating back to her.

*She was in love with someone else.*

Zoe was sure her heart stopped beating. Dead. No. Not like this. He wasn't doing this to her.

'*I'm* her friend,' she said sharply. 'Luke's your friend and Sara's mine, so it's not for you to go to her. That's my job.' It all came out in a rush because she was trying to drown out the little voice in her ear that was telling her things she didn't want to know.

She ran to her cabin, avoiding eye contact with Damien, and started ramming things back in her case. She paid no attention to what was going in or where it was going—much the same way she'd packed on the outbound journey, actually. She yanked her case down off the bunk and dragged it through the main cabin. Damien tried to help her but she pushed past him.

'It was her, wasn't it? The girl who didn't like you back?'

He didn't answer, and when she looked up she found him staring back at her. No words of denial left his lips.

'That's what I thought,' she said and turned to drag her case up on to the first block of the stairway. It was easily a foot and a half high and her case was probably twice the size. She didn't do very well.

Damien was standing right behind her and she let her frustration out on him. She whipped round to face him. 'How could you? He's supposed to be your best friend!'

The shame that washed over his face was all the confirmation she needed.

'It's not like that! At least, it isn't now—'

'I don't want to hear it!' she screamed at him and returned to struggling with her case. At least that way she didn't have to look at him.

It didn't matter about the timing one jot. The fact that he'd *ever* had any kind of feelings for Sara was enough.

The rush of anger produced an adrenalin surge that allowed her to heave her case on to the giant first step. Unfortunately, it didn't stick around long. Not long enough for the second step, anyway.

She felt Damien's warmth behind her, and when he gently eased the handle from her grasp and took it up into the cockpit she didn't fight him.

Instead she sat down on the step and put her face in her hands.

Not again, she screamed inside her head. Not again.

And not with this one. Please.

Damien placed Zoe's hot pink case gently on the pontoon and stood beside it, looking back towards the hatch. The way Zoe had marched past him, case crashing behind her, had somehow prompted a memory of the day his father had left. Angry voices. A door slamming. A sense he'd disappointed someone.

He'd done it again. And he'd have done anything not to see that hurt in Zoe's eyes, to know he'd made her feel that way. In fact, the strength of his own feelings on that front had surprised him. If she'd have let him, he'd have wrapped her in his arms and kissed her anger away, told her things he hadn't even realised had been in his head or heart.

And that hadn't been the only surprise.

The reaching for his car keys had been a knee-jerk reaction. But it wasn't what Zoe had thought. He always jumped in to help out friends in a crisis. It was what he was good at. And Luke and Sara's marriage was in trouble.

When he'd heard Zoe mention her name…
Sara.

For more than a year that one word had prompted a spike of adrenalin that had caused both his heart to race and his stomach to churn. But Damien had a feeling that if he took his pulse right now it would be frighteningly normal. And the only nausea he felt was at hurting Zoe.

He couldn't lie to her. He hadn't ever given her anything less than the truth and he wasn't going to stop now. And he couldn't pretend he'd hadn't felt what he'd felt. Once.

A long breath escaped his lips.

His prayers had been answered. The curse had been lifted. He didn't feel that way about Sara any more. It was such a relief. He'd hoped he'd reached that place, but his reaction to Zoe's phone call was hard evidence.

He needed to tell Zoe, to explain, make her understand. After all, he hadn't done anything wrong, even though it had felt that way sometimes.

Seconds ticked by. He kept staring at the hatch. Eventually he climbed back on board and went to look for her.

She was sitting on the bottom step, fingertips

thrusting through her red curls as she buried her face in her hands. He jumped down beside her, missing most of the steps, and landed hard on the cabin floor. Then he crouched down beside her and looked into her eyes.

She sat up straight, folded her hands in her lap and stared back at him. She was angry. He understood that too.

He reached out to touch her hand and she flinched away. A flicker of something—disgust, maybe—passed across her expression and she looked away to the far end of the cabin.

'I don't think dinner tonight is such a good idea after all,' she said, her voice low and wavering. When she finished talking she risked a glance in his direction to gauge his reaction.

'Zoe, everything's changed—'

She shook her head, silencing him. 'I can't, Damien. Not now.' She looked away. 'And this never was supposed to be anything more than a holiday thing. We should stick to the plan and not make a drama out of something so insignificant.'

Damien thought he must be hearing things. Drama When Not Required was Zoe's forte. But the stare she gave him was blank, empty, and he knew better than to argue at that moment.

'Thank you for sorting out my case for me,' she said, and then she took herself and her brightly coloured handbag up on deck and off the boat.

Damien stayed where he was. He knew it was no good trying to make people stay when they got that look in their eyes. Maybe she was right. He hadn't really been thinking straight this last week. Hadn't he thought all along that they weren't the best match? Perhaps it was better to let her go now rather than discover that he couldn't be happy with her later. Better stop now, before they both got in too deep. He'd seen what that kind of rejection had done to his mother.

No.

The word entered his head and lodged there, refused to budge.

Okay, he hadn't planned on being with someone like Zoe, but he wasn't ready to give up hope yet. They'd had something. Exactly what, he wasn't sure, but he wasn't ready to give up without finding out. There was one last thing he needed to know before he let her go back to London alone.

She was almost on top of the ramp that linked the pontoon to dry land when he caught up with her.

'Zoe!' he yelled from the bottom of the slope.

She turned to look at him, anger in the set of her jaw, hope in her eyes. He walked towards her, gathering both his breath and his thoughts.

'Who was the friend—the bridesmaid—the one your fiancé fell in love with?'

His heart pounded the moment the words left his lips because he feared he already knew the answer.

Zoe's eyes filled with tears. 'Sara,' she said. 'It was Sara.'

And then she turned and walked away, her suitcase whining in pain as she dragged it behind her.

## CHAPTER THIRTEEN

FIVE hours later Zoe was knocking on a faceless hotel door with the sound of low-flying planes ringing in her ears. Sara opened the door. Her eyes were pink and her hair was only about one quarter in her ponytail. The rest was either falling lank or sticking up at odd angles, as if she'd been flopped on the bed sobbing for hours.

Zoe pulled Sara into a hug then guided her back into the room, an arm round her shoulders. Sara's knees buckled and she landed on the end of the bed, making it shudder. Since Zoe wanted to maintain contact, she had no choice but to go with her.

'Oh, Zo! It's such a mess!'

'What happened?'

Sara shook her head, as if she couldn't believe the images running through it. 'I don't know... It seems like it happened to someone else. It started with an argument—a really stupid one about not tying a fender on properly—but then it just got way out of control.'

'But you're going to be okay, right? You and Luke?'

Sara just pressed the heels of her hands into her eye sockets and juddered. Zoe laid her cheek on her friend's shoulder and rubbed her back until the silent tears slowed.

Sara's voice was muffled through her hands. 'You should have heard the things we said to each other! And then I…I just…snapped, I suppose. I told him if he really felt that way he'd have been better off not marrying me and then I went to the nearest telephone and booked a flight home.' Another shudder racked her body, and she looked up at Zoe with swollen eyes and sticky lashes.

'That was a bit dramatic.'

Sara's shoulders slumped further. 'I know! I've never done anything remotely like it before. It was just…just…' She suddenly sat up straighter and looked Zoe in the eye. 'What if he won't forgive me? I've been so horrible! How can I ever repair this?'

Zoe hugged Sara, a slight smile on her lips. 'Of course he'll forgive you. He loves you, remember? And you've both been under such stress getting this wedding together. I wouldn't be surprised if honeymoons weren't a bit like Christmas with the family,' she added.

Sara looked up at her, confused.

Of course she wouldn't know. The rest of her family were all as lovely as she was.

'You know… Everyone wants it to be perfect, but all those tensions that have been building all year have a habit of coming to the surface just when you don't want them to.'

That was how it was in Zoe's house, anyway. Her grandmother said they hadn't had a proper Christmas if at least one bit of crockery wasn't smashed and the front door didn't slam every half hour with the latest dramatic exit.

Sara dragged her hand across her eyes, then got up to retrieve a tissue from the box on the rather functional dressing table. 'Maybe… I did so want our honeymoon to be perfect.'

Zoe made a wry face. 'That's a lot of pressure to put on one man and a boat.'

Sara sighed and sat down on the top end of the bed, pulling her legs up and propping herself against the headboard. 'In the run-up to getting married you're supposed to be the picture of blissful happiness, aren't you? So all the little things that are irritating you, well, you stuff them away, hide them. At least I did.' She blew out a long breath. 'I suppose there's a lot of pressure involved in being a bride, too.'

There was the way Sara had gone about it, Zoe thought. She scooted up the mattress to join Sara at the top end. 'It got to you, huh? You should have said something. I'd have understood. Been there myself, after all.'

'I didn't want to remind you.' Sara rolled her head sideways on the headboard to look at her. 'But more than that, I suppose I thought if I said it out loud at all that I'd ruin everything. I know what people think about me, what they say about me, they expect a certain standard. I felt my wedding had to live up to that.'

'Nobody's perfect,' Zoe said. And didn't she know that more than most? But it was refreshing to know that Sara felt the same pressure to perform, that Zoe wasn't the only one of the pair who could mess up badly. That realisation changed something. Suddenly Zoe felt older, stronger. More free.

'You need to tell Luke all of this,' she said to her friend. 'He's probably feeling the same way.'

'You think?'

Zoe nodded and let out a low chuckle. 'I think what you should have done is have a massive row on day three, get it all out of your system, and then have mind-blowing make-up sex.'

Sara pulled a glum face. 'But I got on a plane and came home! How are we going to get over that?'

Zoe reached over and patted Sara's leg. 'Listen, I'm the queen of impulsive bad choices and if there's one thing I've learned it's that nothing is so awful that it can't be sorted out somehow. It just takes a bit of guts, a bit of humility—and *a lot* of grovelling.'

Sara let out a watery laugh. 'Thanks, Zo. You always cheer me up, stop me taking myself too seriously. I don't know what I'd do without you. And I'm so sorry I messed up the end of your holiday too.' She gave Zoe a sideways look. The sort of look that begged information. 'How was it going?' she asked innocently.

Ah, yes. In all the drama, Zoe had forgotten about that. Time to get some answers while Sara was calmer.

'Why on earth did you set Damien and me up like that?'

Sara sighed. 'We didn't. At least not on purpose.'

Zoe crossed her arms. 'Convince me.'

'Luke and I had chatted about giving someone
else the use of the boat, and I instantly assumed
he meant Damien—after all, he borrows *Weaver*
a couple of times a year anyway. So, when I had
a chance, I talked to Damien. I had no idea Luke
had mentioned it to you until the next day.'

'And when you realised you instantly rang me
to let me know about the mix up?' Zoe said sar-
castically.

'Luke told me about what he saw in the garden,
you know…' Sara's voice was low and she nudged
Zoe's leg with her foot.

Zoe stared straight ahead and kept her voice
light and unconcerned. 'Oh, he did, did he?'

'So, when we realised we'd, well, double-booked
the pair of you, we thought maybe it wasn't such
a bad idea after all.'

In the following silence she knew Sara was waiting for her to spill her guts, as they always did
about every romantic encounter, but Zoe wasn't
ready to talk about Damien. Not by a long shot.
And especially not with Sara.

She should have guessed, shouldn't she? Damien

had plans, he always wanted the best, everything to be perfect. Why hadn't she realised that would apply to his romantic life as well as things like sailing and business? As soon as she looked at it that way, Sara became the natural choice.

And Zoe was so obviously not.

'He isn't for me,' she said eventually.

*Not for you, either*, she silently added. *But he's going to have to work that one out on his own.*

'Rubbish!' Sara replied, obviously distracting herself from the mess of her own life by meddling with Zoe's. 'Damien's got a great job, he's successful, he's a fantastic friend to Luke—the sort of guy who'd never let you down—and he's...well, he's seriously hot.' She blushed a little as she said this, and Zoe felt slightly nauseous. 'He's practically perfect. What's not to like? Especially if he likes you too?'

'Nobody's perfect,' Zoe said again.

And she knew that for sure now, had discovered that elusive kryptonite that'd bring so-called Mr Perfect to his knees. She felt as if he'd lied to her, as if he'd betrayed all three of them somehow, even though she knew instinctively that he'd have never acted on whatever he felt.

Oh, why couldn't the mystery in his past, the

one woman who hadn't wanted him back, been a nameless, faceless thing? Why did it have to be her best friend?

She swung her legs off the bed, fetched Sara's handbag from the desk and handed it to her. 'You need to phone your husband.'

Sara looked at her handbag as if it were about to swallow her whole. 'I'm scared,' she said in a small voice.

'I know.' Zoe sat down beside her on the edge of the bed. 'But I'm here with you.' She dropped the bag in her friend's lap. 'And you love each other. This is just the first of many bumps in the road of a long and happy marriage.'

Sara nodded. Just once. 'When did you become so wise?' she asked quietly, and then she reached into her handbag and pulled out her phone.

He'd thought she'd calm down and that he'd be able to go and see her, to explain, after a few days. Just showed how flawed *that* plan had been. In the month since they'd returned from Devon, Zoe hadn't answered one of his calls. He'd got her email address from Luke but she wouldn't answer any of those either. It was only the fact that he knew he'd have an opportunity to see her tonight that had stopped him going to her flat and banging down her front door.

Not a good idea. He knew that Zoe's response to conflict was to throw more petrol on the fire. It seemed Damien Stone was finally all out of good plans.

He stood at Luke and Sara's front door and stared at the brass knocker. He wasn't sure this was a brilliant idea, either. A thank you dinner for the best man and maid of honour. It could just turn out to be Round Two.

Luke and Sara had patched things up, but their honeymoon disaster had given them both quite a scare. When Luke had phoned him, telling him the full details of what had happened, he'd hardly been able to believe it. Not Sara. Sara didn't do that kind of thing.

Only she obviously did. Because she had.

And any remaining pieces of the idol Damien had created in her image had crumbled. She was still his friend, and she was still lovely, but he no longer elevated her to goddess status. He really had let go. Of Sara. Of even the idea of Sara. None of it had been real, anyway.

Unfortunately, he wasn't sure he could make Zoe see it that way.

He had a suspicion the newlyweds, now they were happily reunited, were trying to do a bit of matchmaking. He didn't know if Zoe had confided in Sara, but he hadn't said anything to Luke about what had gone on between them. His best friend had been putting his fledgling marriage back together—the last thing he'd needed was to get embroiled in someone else's romantic problems.

He shifted the bunch of flowers he'd brought for the hostess into the same hand that was gripping a bottle of wine and knocked on the door. It was opened moments later by a smiling Sara, wearing a floral apron, her hair caught up in a messy ponytail at the back of her head. She kissed his cheek, relieved him of flowers and wine, and led him through the house and into the kitchen.

'Luke's barbecuing,' she said, smiling as she put the wine down on the counter. 'Go and do man-stuff out there. You know, keep him company while he grunts at the fire.' She nodded in the direction of the French windows leading into the courtyard garden.

So Zoe wasn't here yet, then. Damien wasn't sure whether to be disappointed or relieved he had more time to prepare himself. His heart began to thud.

He'd missed her. Really missed her. And it was more than just being sorry about the way things had ended. Somehow his life seemed...empty. It was as if the sunshine had stayed in Devon, even though London had delivered the cloudless skies of an Indian summer well into September.

He stepped into the garden and greeted his friend with a hug. For that he was rewarded with a bottle of beer. It was only when he couldn't find a bottle opener on the garden table that he looked up and saw her, standing by the ivy-covered wall, a glass of white wine gripped between even whiter fingers.

Once again he had the sensation of being hit by a truck. But this time it didn't stop there: it ran him over, then backed up and made mincemeat of him.

Zoe was wearing that sundress she'd had on the night she'd got sunburned—a favourite of his ever since. Her untidy curls had been tamed into a twist at the back of her head, but escapee tendrils framed her face and curled at her nape. He didn't think he'd ever seen her look more beautiful.

'Hi,' he croaked, and he didn't even notice when

Sara gently prised his beer bottle from his hand, took the cap off and handed it back to him.

Zoe looked at him, head tilted down a little, with her eyes wide and her mouth thin. 'Hi.' The word shot from her mouth like a bullet.

Direct hit, Damien thought. Just hearing her voice, as cold and wary as it was, made his chest contract.

Dinner was painful. Uncomfortable. At least it was for the two unmarried guests. Luke and Sara were definitely experiencing a second wind of newly wedded bliss. Unfortunately, their loved-up state made them impervious to the awkwardness of their guests, especially when the hosts dropped hints about holiday romances and fountains in hotel gardens.

Zoe's biting wit was at its finest, and more than once he found himself as her bullseye. He took it. He'd rather see her fighting than crumbling, and in the silences in between the barbs he saw the look of raw hurt in her eyes.

Sara swallowed a mouthful of wine as they finished up their main course. 'Tell Damien about your expansion plans,' she said to Zoe.

Zoe fidgeted in her seat. She really didn't want to talk about this. Not with Damien here, because he'd been the one to start her thinking on this track, to make her realise that her business was never going to grow unless she stopped daydreaming and did something about it.

'I'm leasing one of the little shops on the fringes of Greenwich market,' she said. 'Not quite a rival to Tiffany's yet, but it's a start.'

'She's got a bank loan and everything, haven't you, Zoe?' Sara added excitedly.

Zoe rolled her eyes at her friend and nodded. When she looked back over the table at Damien, the look of pride in his eyes and the soft smile on his lips almost undid all her resolution to remain aloof and distant.

'I'm glad,' was all he said.

It was enough. Zoe didn't want to feel all warm and fuzzy at his words. She didn't want to feel anything about him at all, thank you very much.

Sara went on to talk about how much she loved Zoe's dinky new premises, how much fun they were going to have repainting the display cases of what had been an old-fashioned gentlemen's haberdashery store. Zoe didn't listen. She was watching Damien, just like she'd been watching him all evening, waiting for something—a flash in his eyes, a facial tic—when he looked at Sara that would confirm all her worst fears.

And there was one expression in particular she feared the most, and every time she felt herself weakening she made herself remember that look—the one he'd worn as he'd watched Sara walk down the aisle. It haunted her now, in painful and exquisite detail. She hadn't seen it tonight yet, but that didn't mean he wouldn't slip up one day.

Nobody could survive a relationship with that hanging over them. It would be a miserable way to live. It certainly was a miserable way to love.

Dessert was served as the sky became fully dark and Sara turned on the string of lights that decorated the little pergola in her tiny paved garden. Zoe pushed her cheesecake around her plate for a while, but decided she had to at least eat some of it. If she didn't, Sara would know that something was wrong, and she really didn't want an inquisition to start while she was sitting opposite Damien. Tonight had been hard enough as it was.

Hard, because she knew that just a slight move of her foot would have brought it into contact with his. Just a reach for the salt at the same time would have caused their fingers to brush. A million little ways she could engineer her own undoing.

She wanted to touch him so badly that she was scared she'd sabotage herself and do it anyway. She needed to get out of here.

She looked up just after she'd put the first spoonful in her mouth, habitually turning it over so she could capture every speck of dessert with her tongue, and discovered Damien staring at her. The lump of cheesecake that had been dangling on the end of his fork slid on to his plate with a splat. He didn't even react.

Sara gave her husband a not-so-subtle thumbs-up sign across the table.

Zoe noticed a humming in her ears as static electricity crawled up her arms and made her body tingle. She pulled the spoon slowly out of her mouth and placed it carefully back down on her plate. Everyone watched her. Everyone was quiet.

She pushed her chair back from the table. 'Thanks for the lovely evening, you two,' she said quickly, looking down and catching nobody's eye. 'But I'm afraid I have to get going. I pick up the keys to the shop bright and early in the morning.'

The hosts were instantly on their feet. 'But we've still got cheese and biscuits to come,' Sara said mournfully. 'Stay for that, at least.' But she wasn't looking at the cheeseboard sitting in the middle of the table when she said it. She was looking at Damien.

Zoe shook her head. 'Sorry.' Her impulse had been to get out of there, and she was going with it.

Sara ran to get Zoe's cardigan. 'Well, at least let us call you a cab.'

Zoe huffed. 'I live five minutes away. Don't be ridiculous. I'll be fine walking.'

'But it's dark,' Sara added, and then she narrowed her eyes and looked from Zoe to Damien and back again. 'Luke will walk you back.'

Luke was visibly, and almost audibly, surprised by the suggestion, but one look from his wife silenced him. He shrugged and headed for the door.

Zoe started to relax slightly as she and Sara said their goodbyes by the front door, talking over the top of each other and promising to call the following day. Luke rolled his eyes and told them to get on with it, and Damien stood back and watched. She could tell his eyes didn't leave her for a second, even though she was never brave enough to meet his gaze.

A few more seconds and she'd be able to breathe again. The front door would shut behind her, blocking him from her view, and she wouldn't have to see him for another few months, hopefully, and by then she'd be better. Stronger. Over him.

But she should have accounted for Sara's more devious side, a trait that had been coming more and more to the fore in recent weeks. Just as Zoe and Luke were about to leave, Sara grabbed her husband's arm.

'Actually, even better…' she dragged him back inside '…Luke can help me clear up and Damien can walk you.'

She obviously caught the man in question by surprise too, because, despite her petite frame, she managed to shove him out of the door with no problem and she closed it swiftly behind them before Zoe could argue.

That left her and Damien standing on the front step staring at each other.

Zoe just shook her head and walked down the path. 'I don't want you to walk me home,' she said without looking at him, but knowing he would follow. 'I don't want to be near you at all.'

## CHAPTER FOURTEEN

DAMIEN wasn't about to let Zoe walk away again. Or should that be *run* away? Another sleight of hand of hers, he realised. She'd flee uncomfortable situations, passing the blame to the other party, making them feel as if they'd pushed her, when really the momentum had been hers alone. And it was time to make her stop. Time for her to face what she was running from.

He caught up with her, placed his hands lightly on her shoulders. Much to his surprise, she halted instantly. But she didn't turn, just stared at the cracked paving stone illuminated by the dull orb of light from a street lamp. Rather than turning her towards him, he circled around her, maintaining contact, preventing any forward progress.

He expected to find her glaring back at him, lightning bolts flashing from her eyes ready to sizzle him to a crisp, but instead they were filled with tears. He didn't say anything, just brushed them from under her lashes with his thumbs while her bottom lip wobbled, and then he leaned in close and pressed his lips softly to hers. Just a single kiss, but he couldn't bear to break contact so he stayed there, lips touching hers. Neither of them moved. More tears slid from her closed lids and after a second he tasted their salt.

His brain had just sent a signal to pull away when Zoe stopped him before he'd even begun to move. She placed her palms on his cheeks, held him there while she returned the favour. He could feel her quivering, her hands shaking against his skin.

But finally her mouth left his and she stepped back, ran her tongue across her bottom lip and tasted the damp salt of her own tears before sweeping them away.

She blinked slowly and looked away. 'There's no point, Damien. We both know that.'

He took a step forward. 'There's every point. You don't understand—'

'I understand just fine,' she snapped. 'It was a fling. It's over. That's all.'

'What if I don't want it to be over?'

She stood tall and her chin tilted upwards. 'Then you're fooling yourself. You know I'm not the one you really want.'

That wasn't true. Not any more. But she was so blinkered, so fixed on that one point that she couldn't see anything else. Damien almost felt like laughing. How many times had people accused him of exactly the same thing? But Zoe had been the one who'd shown him a better way, made him realise how badly that approach could short-change a person, how it could rob them of things they'd never even dared to imagine could be theirs.

'I thought you were the one to follow the mad impulses, take chances.' He stepped forward until he was practically nose to nose with her, lowered his voice. 'Take a chance on *me*.'

She bit her lip and her eyes widened further.

'I want *you*, Zoe,' he said quietly, firmly.

She shook her head and took another step backwards. Then she smiled, but it wasn't a pretty smile. A millimetre less width and it would be a grimace of pain.

'I'm not right for you.' Her voice caught. 'Okay, maybe it could be more than a fling, but the fact you want more from me now doesn't change anything in the long run. Eventually you'll stop wanting me and you'll want *her*—or someone like her. They always do.'

He realised then that he wasn't going to get through to her with just talking. He also needed time to think, time to work out if his iron-clad certainty was as solid as he'd thought it was. He was very good at setting things in stone and then pursuing them blindly, wasn't he? Sometimes without asking if he was following the right path.

'Can you guarantee me you'll never look at her and wonder *what if*?' she asked, her expression hard now. 'Or that you won't regret choosing me instead?'

Two minutes ago he would have said yes in a heartbeat. But was there truth in what she'd just said? Would he, like his father, wake up one day and discover the life—the woman—he'd chosen wasn't enough? He didn't want to even consider that option, but he owed it to Zoe to be certain. He couldn't let her fall in love with him and then snatch it all away from her. She'd already had that done to her once.

He reached his hand out and let it drop down by his side again. 'No, I can't. Not yet.'

Another tear fell. She let it roll until it reached her chin and then she wiped it away with the heel of her hand. She walked around him, stepping off the kerb to give him a wide berth, and when

she was back on the pavement again she turned
to look at him.

'Then I can't take a chance on you, Damien. You
know that. I can't be your backup plan. She will
always be the one you picked first and I can't live
with that.' She started walking backwards, away
from him, away from the glow of the street light.
'There's nothing we can do to change that, and
I'm afraid it's a deal-breaker for me.'

And then she turned and walked away. Damien
waited a while then followed her, his feet heavy.
There wasn't anything else he could say. Not tonight. He kept at a discreet distance, made sure
she was safe until she walked up the path to her
front door, where she gave him one last look as
she turned her key, then went inside, shutting the
glossy red door firmly behind her.

Zoe slumped against the back of her front door
and let the rest of her tears fall. She pressed her
hands against her face as if she could somehow
stop herself from falling apart by that one simple
action.

He'd broken her heart. How had he done that
when she'd been so careful not to give it to him?
It wasn't fair.

She had known she was right, but she hadn't wanted to be. Right about Sara, right about there being no possibility of a future for them, but it had killed her to hear him agree.

The building was little more than a shell of girders. Damien stood at the edge of the site overlooking the Thames, the sound of bulldozers droning in his ears, and stared out at the water. He was normally really excited at this stage of a project. After months of preparation, it was time to start making those plans a reality.

For days now he'd been preoccupied with trying to work out the answer to Zoe's question. For days now he'd failed miserably. How could you predict something like that? Inside his head he'd taken his mental jigsaw puzzle and arranged it a hundred different ways. He'd shuffled pieces around, trying to create a space that Zoe would fit into, so he could give her the assurances she wanted. It had been no use. It had always felt as if he was jamming that last piece unnaturally into a gap that it didn't really belong in, and that scared him.

The only option had been to pull the whole thing apart, piece by piece, and scramble it up. All the bits were sitting at the fringes of his consciousness now, out of order, and it was driving him crazy.

He had one piece left in his hands. Zoe.

The site foreman came to him with a question and Damien reeled off an answer on autopilot. Then he called the man back and checked the details again.

'Sorry,' he said. 'Just needed to be sure.'

The man shrugged. 'No problem. It's your money we'll be pouring down the toilet if we get it wrong, and at the stage when we have to make sure the structure is right. Otherwise there's no point adding to it.'

Damien nodded and the man wandered off with his clipboard. When he was alone again he went back to his mental riddle.

Start with the thing that needs to be there to make the whole thing work. Start with the foundation.

Just like his idea of the perfect woman, his idea of the perfect future was an illusion too. He swept those pieces away.

Nothing and nobody was perfect in this world, but maybe that was okay. Maybe there was beauty and happiness to be found in it anyway. Maybe it was about appreciating what was right in front of you, instead of always wishing for something more—something his father had yet to learn to do. Something Zoe's bonehead fiancé had thankfully also done.

He took that one piece of the jigsaw he still held in his hands and put it front and centre in an empty space. Then he shooed all the other little bits away that tried to gather round and crowd it.

There was no perfect picture he could make for Zoe. But he'd been looking at it the wrong way. This was a jigsaw with only one piece. The rest would come later. He'd build it around her whichever way it fitted, be the edges messy or undefined, and he didn't care. All he knew was that he couldn't imagine his life without her in it.

Now he just had to make her believe it too.

Zoe leaned into the compact shop window that faced on to the covered hall of Greenwich market and hung a necklace on a display stand. It was her usual style: big chunky wooden beads with different colours and grains, mixed with chunky silver shapes and multi-faceted glass beads. This one was all in shades of pale beige, yellow and blue. It reminded her of the Cornish coast on a sunny day when the heat haze had risen.

Outside, the market was coming to life. Traders were filling their stalls with their wares. Today was Thursday, so it was vintage fashion and hand-made toys, antiques and precious stones. Quite a few early shoppers had already drifted past and stopped at her window display. She hoped that boded well.

She'd only opened last Saturday, so it was early days yet, but she'd done okay so far. She hoped it wasn't just the novelty of a new shop and that business would continue to grow, but who knew what would happen in the future? She'd planned it out with the help of a financial adviser. The only thing to do now was hold her breath and see if she pulled it off. If she was still open this time next year she'd give herself permission to exhale.

The best way to check a window display was to see it the way the customers did—from the out-side—so Zoe did just that. She stood, hands on hips, a good six feet away from her window and tipped her head to one side.

The display included colourful necklaces, brace-lets and earrings. She didn't think she could fit much else in the window without overcrowding it, yet at the same time it looked empty. Something was missing. A gnawing sensation in her stomach reminded her exactly what that was.

She knew the delicate, interwoven silver designs she'd drawn on the boat would look perfect interspersed amongst the larger pieces. Pity she didn't have any to put there. Not because she'd sold them, but because they were still just doodles in her sketchpad. Imaginations.

She had the materials in her safe. She had the right tools for the job. She just lacked the guts. Partly because every time she looked at them she thought of Damien, but more because she was scared that they wouldn't turn out the way she wanted them to, that she couldn't actually pull all that intricate work off.

And now would be a really good time to pull something special out of the bag. Yesterday she'd got an email from someone wanting to commission a wedding and engagement ring set. Something unusual, the client had said. He'd given her carte blanche. And Mr Peters wanted it all kept very hush-hush because it was going to be a surprise for the lucky lady.

She had a little workbench near the till at the back of the shop and she returned to it now, pulled her leather sketchpad out from its shelf and looked at it. She left it open on the desk and went to the back room-slash-office where her safe was. She returned with a pouch containing a square-cut emerald. This stone for the engagement ring, she'd decided, although she didn't know why. It was something she'd picked up for a good price a couple of years ago, but had never really made anything it could fit into before now.

She unwrapped the stone from its little pouch as she walked back on to the tiny shop floor, eyes down. When she looked up again she almost threw both pouch and stone into the air.

A large, dark shape was filling her doorway. It was Damien, looking impossibly delicious in an immaculately cut suit.

'You did it,' was all he said, looking round and smiling.

Zoe was shaking. How was he standing there looking all normal and sounding all calm? She nodded, since her head was inclined to wobble with the rest of her.

'I knew you could,' he added. 'You just needed to believe it too.'

She nodded again, not even really sure what she was agreeing with.

'What are you doing here?' she finally said.

'Luke told me you'd opened your shop. I wanted to stop by and wish you well.' He handed her a small gift-wrapped package. 'I thought this might come in handy.'

Zoe took it from him. It would be rude not to. And instantly recognised the contours of her favourite brand of 'emergency' chocolate through the wrapping paper.

'Setting up a business can be stressful,' he said, a slight smile tugging the corner of his mouth. 'A little red box with breakable glass and a hammer might be a good idea.'

Zoe dropped the chocolate on the counter by the till and closed her eyes. Why hadn't she leased a bigger shop? She was right at the back, and he was only a pace or so away from the door and already he was too close. She closed her eyes and her voice grew thin. 'Don't be nice to me... Just don't.'

She heard him close the distance between them and opened her eyes in panic, just as he stopped in front of her and took the emerald from her fingers. 'Lovely stone.'

She nodded again. She really must stop doing that. Otherwise she'd have to get herself a part-time job sitting on the parcel shelf of somebody's car. 'They're my favourite.'

He held it up to the light. 'I had a great-aunt who hated emeralds. She married a diamond broker, and after that she got very particular about her jewellery. She thought emeralds were second class. Something about impurities and flaws.'

'She's right. Emeralds are actually a type of beryl—which are a totally different colour—but impurities in the stone turn it green. They're notorious for their flaws, too.'

He handed it back to her and looked her in the eye. 'Doesn't stop them being beautiful.'

'No.' She gulped down a breath. Were they still talking about emeralds?

He kept looking her straight in the eye until she had to turn away. 'Why are you really here?' she asked. 'This isn't about chocolate.'

He put his hands in his pockets and frowned. 'I thought a lot about what you said, about whether I could give you a guarantee.'

Her breathing became all light and fluttery. 'Can you?'

'No. I can't promise you a perfect future, Zoe.' He reached out and touched her face. 'But I don't think anyone can make a promise like that to someone else. Life is like sailing—you do your best to plot your course, and then you weather the conditions together, dealing with whatever is thrown at you. And I think you and I make a good team.'

She shook her hand away and stepped back. Oh, they were persuasive words, and she so wanted to believe him because she knew he meant what he was saying. But it wouldn't change anything: Aiden had worn that very same earnest look on his face the night he'd asked her to marry him.

'Maybe we do make a good team.' She shook her head, backed away a little further behind the counter. 'But I can't be your sidekick, Damien. The consolation prize who trots along beside you, while everyone else wonders why you're with her. A relationship with unequal partners just won't work.'

His jaw tensed and his eyes narrowed slightly. She was making him cross. Good. That was much better than the heartfelt looks he'd been giving her. She could handle cross.

'This sidekick thing is all rubbish,' he said in that imperious manner that used to make her want to scream.

'Oh, it is, is it? Well, I doubt you've ever been

on the receiving end of that kind of treatment, so how would you know?'

He let out a dry laugh, not a pleasant sound. 'Really? Then answer me one question—and I know we've been here before—but when the joke's on me, what do they say?'

'That you're always the best man,' she said slowly, expecting this to be a trick question, which it might be.

'Exactly. Seven times now. That has to be a record. So I don't want to hear any of this sidekick versus leading man nonsense, okay?'

Zoe frowned. 'I don't see how the two are connected.'

'The best man isn't the leading man on a wedding day—the groom is—and I've never been the groom. So that would make *me* the sidekick.'

Zoe's eyes grew wide. He so clearly wasn't. 'That's impossible. You can't be.'

'No, I'm not. And neither are you, but you can't see it.' He shook his head in exasperation. 'You're right. A relationship won't work with unequal partners. But I'm not the one who believes you're second class, Zoe. It's you.'

No, that wasn't right. That couldn't be right. It was other people who labelled her, who treated like that. All she'd ever wanted was for someone to pick her first, make her their top choice. Damien had been like all the rest.

'You're dreaming,' she said, 'if you think that.'

He reached over to the small work desk and picked up the sketchbook lying there. 'I know I'm dreaming,' he said. 'But it's not wrong to hope. It's not dangerous. And some dreams are meant to come true.' He showed the sketchpad to her. 'That's what designs are, aren't they? Dreams on paper. A vision of something that hasn't become real yet.'

She frowned and took the pad from him, held it to her chest.

'I *know* we can be good together—' he tapped his finger to his temple '—I can see it. But I can't force you to take a chance on me. I can't make you believe that it's you that I want and not anyone else,' he said as he turned and walked towards the door. 'But make those, Zoe. Let yourself dream about *something*, because you're going to be miserable until you do.'

# CHAPTER FIFTEEN

Zoe put the ring she was working on down and slumped back in her chair. Her secretive client wanted something unique, something one-of-a-kind and, since Zoe had been in the creative doldrums ever since she'd returned from Devon, she'd had no choice but to go back to those designs and tweak them a little. It had nothing to do with what Damien had said when he'd visited the shop the week before last, nothing at all.

It was a wedding ring, white gold. Unlike Sara's, which had been clean lines and elegant curves, this was an intricate design of interwoven strands, inspired by climbing ivy, old Art Nouveau posters and Celtic knotwork. The vision she had for the end product was stunning, but getting it right was driving her crazy. It was rough around the edges now but, if she looked carefully, she could envisage the finished version shimmering tantalisingly beneath the surface, just out of reach. She stuffed the ring into a pouch where it couldn't mock her.

She'd agreed to meet Sara for cocktails in a local wine bar and it was almost time to get going. Privately, she thought Sara was turning into a bit of a mother hen, fussing round her and asking her if she was eating properly. Seriously, when had anyone ever worried about that on Zoe's account? She was sure this was just another of Sara's mercy missions to cheer her single friend up. But maybe it was better than sitting here and getting frustrated with strips of fine metal that wouldn't consent to sit right.

The old-fashioned shop bell she'd recently fitted above the door jangled and she looked up to find Sara walking towards her. 'Normal people are shutting up shop and going home for the day,' she said. 'Ready for that Monday night cocktail?'

Zoe put the ring down and pushed her hands above her head to stretch out the kinks in her shoulders. 'Just a quick one. After that I'm going to take these home and try to finish them off. I've got to deliver them to a hotel in central London late Friday afternoon. It's all very cloak and dagger.'

'It's stunning, Zo,' Sara said, picking up the ring and examining it. 'Where's the engagement ring?'

She opened up a midnight blue velvet box sitting on the bench beside her and turned it to face her friend. Sara's mouth dropped open. 'Wow.'

Zoe smiled to herself. 'That was the effect I was hoping it would have.'

'I've never seen anything quite like it. All those twisting little strands, and that lone emerald right in the middle. It's very *you*, somehow.' She handed the box back to Zoe, then hoisted her handbag even further up on her shoulder. 'Ready?'

Zoe shook her head and began to pack away her things. 'Almost.'

She put the display pieces from the window into the safe and went round turning off lights and tidying up. With Sara's help, it was only ten minutes before she was locking the shop door behind her and pulling down the metal grille.

Even though it was still fairly early, Monday night happy hour was in full swing at the wine bar. Lots of young professionals either rounding off a good weekend or commiserating on the start of a new working week, probably. They found themselves stools near the bar and Zoe ordered herself something fun-looking and toxic, while Sara stuck to a tried-and-tested margarita. They chatted about silly, inconsequential matters as they sipped their drinks.

Things had been different between her and Sara since what they now referred to as The Honeymoon Meltdown. Zoe no longer felt like the geek who'd somehow managed to slide into the in-crowd unnoticed. She'd been guilty of believing Sara's life was perfect, when clearly she suffered from the same insecurities as everyone else. Maybe her friend would have been able to talk to her about how stressed she'd been in the run up to the wedding if Zoe hadn't also unconsciously put her on a pedestal too, adding to the pressure.

She sucked on her straw and took a sideways look at her best friend. Hmm. Putting Sara on a pedestal. Seemed she had more in common with Damien than she'd realised. And if she'd managed to change, could he?

She sighed. Damien. He hadn't contacted her in the last two weeks. So she supposed he'd finally given up, which was a shame because she'd spent a lot of time thinking about what he'd said.

He'd dared her to dream, hadn't he? And she had—by signing the lease on her little shop, by working on the designs that she knew would take her business to a new level. Now she'd stopped just reacting to the situation, to him and all the feelings his secret had churned up, she could see he'd been right. It was hard work, and it didn't always go according to plan, but the gamble was worth it. She was happier now. Professionally, at least. Personally, she was still pretty miserable.

Maybe it was time to do something about that. Maybe it was time to peel off that 'sidekick' label she'd stuck on her own forehead, because he'd been right about that too. And she had the funny feeling that sense of imbalance, of not being able to talk to her as an equal—because she wouldn't let him—might have been part of the reason Aiden had looked elsewhere. Oh, he was still a rat, she didn't doubt that, but maybe things weren't quite as black and white as she'd once thought.

Before she knew it, her glass was empty. Just as well she was getting the bus home.

Sara's eyes widened and she knocked back the rest of her cocktail to keep up. 'Another?'

Zoe shook her head. 'You run along home to your lovely new husband. Stop worrying about me.'

Sara grimaced. 'Busted,' she said.

'Besides,' Zoe added, 'I have a ring I need to finish.'

* * *

Zoe stared at the bit of paper in her hands and frowned. The address she'd been given was the name of a hotel, but this was little more than a building site. A truck drove past her, through deep brown mud, and disappeared through the gate made of dark green chipboard.

The ring box was in her jacket pocket and she absently played with its corners, finding its cuboid shape comforting. All that work. And this was… what? A hoax? One that had cost her money she couldn't afford in both time and materials.

She noticed a man in a hard hat walking towards her.

'Miss St James?'

She nodded, almost perplexed by the fact he knew her name, even though this was where she'd been told to come.

'If you'd like to come with me?'

He handed her a matching yellow hat and waited for her to jam it on top of her curls. Fabulous. It had taken hours to shop for an outfit to impress this obviously high-end client, and now this hat was going to make her look like a duck.

The man led her to one of those lifts that were really just a cage, and up they shot into the sky. Zoe hadn't realised the building was so tall. It was mostly steel girders and concrete floors. Here and there on the bottom levels things were taking more shape, but when she stepped out of the lift a minute later she could feel the early autumn breeze on her face and see the glint of the Thames way below.

Zoe held tightly on to the ring box in her pocket. This was some sort of dream, wasn't it? She was probably hallucinating. But the clang of the lift as it disappeared back down towards the ground sounded real enough. As did the gurgling of her nervous stomach.

Why had he left her alone up here?

But then she realised she wasn't alone. On the far side of a vast concrete floor a man was silhouetted against the late afternoon sun. She shielded her eyes with her hand and began to walk towards him, glad she was moving away from the edge.

'Mr Peters?'

He turned, and Zoe's quivering stomach followed the recently departed lift. He started moving towards her, crossing the rough concrete floor in long strides. Slowly, as he stepped more into the gloom of the inner building, her eyes began to adjust, make out his features…

And then it wasn't the mysterious Mr Peters walking towards her but Damien.

Why was he…? How had he…?

Oh. She got it now. One of her brothers was called Peter, so she knew it came from the Greek word for stone. Very clever. Also very devious.

But why the charade? What did it mean? She felt as if something inside her wanted to fly. She held it tight, terrified of what might happen if she let it.

Don't cry, she told herself. Don't be that pathetic. You came here to do a job, so do it. Keep it dignified.

She pulled the box from her pocket and held it out to him. He didn't smile. He didn't say anything. In fact, he had an intense, slightly pained expression on his face that she knew she'd seen before. She just couldn't remember where.

'Your rings,' she said. That was all she'd meant to say, but then she heard herself add, 'You found a replacement for Sara pretty quick.'

Outwardly, she kept her expression neutral. Inwardly, she was kicking herself and reminding herself, not very gently, that she was supposed to be thinking before she spoke, not just firing off words in reaction to any uncomfortable emotion.

'Sorry,' she added. 'That was a stupid thing to say.'

Damien's expression was still unreadable. 'I don't want to replace Sara.'

She hadn't realised she'd let go of that fluttering thing inside her and that hope had been soaring quietly in her heart until that moment. It fell to the ground like a bird shot with an arrow.

Still stuck on Sara. Why had she expected anything else? It was the pattern of her romantic relationships up until now, after all. For the first time in her life, Zoe wondered if she'd have to cut her best friend out of her life if she was ever going to have a chance at love, something she really didn't want to do.

Damien opened the box and stared at the delicate twisting rings nestled together in their blue cushion. Although the lid obscured Zoe's view, she knew both pieces so intimately that she followed his gaze in her imagination, tracing every line and curve. He didn't speak for a long time.

'They're beautiful,' he said quietly. 'Even more than I'd imagined they would be.'

That had been Zoe's reaction when she'd finally finished them too—especially the wedding ring. She could hardly believe her hands had crafted it.

Zoe folded her arms across her front, vainly hoping it would somehow halt the rising glow of gratification his words had produced inside her.

'There's only one woman who can wear this ring,' he said as he looked up at her, and Zoe had a flash of realisation so strong she stopped breathing.

She could label that expression now. It was like the one she'd been waiting for all evening when they'd had dinner at Luke and Sara's. The one she'd seen on his face when he'd been looking past her up the aisle at Sara. Like it, but not the same. More like its big brother. More intense. More real.

That bird, the one that Zoe was sure had been shot dead, suddenly rose like a phoenix and started flapping around all over the place inside her chest. She checked over her shoulder, just to make sure no one was standing behind her, but they were all alone.

Nobody was there. Sara wasn't there.

So it must be *her* he was looking at with raw longing in his eyes.

Zoe wished that a chair would materialise from somewhere. She really needed to sit down.

'Without her my life is empty, boring—full of straight lines and tick boxes.' He looked down at the open ring box in his hand and turned it to face her. 'I want my life to be like this ring. It has form and structure, but it's also surprising and exceptional. So, no, I don't want a replacement for Sara. The woman I would like to wear this ring is one of a kind.'

Zoe's hand flew to her chest. She could feel her heart pumping a wild jig beneath her fingers. Oh, she so wanted to believe him.

'I don't know...'

Damien placed the box in her hands. The square of velvet was warm against her palm.

'I don't think we're cast at birth in certain roles—some always destined to fly, some always destined to be second in line. When it comes to love it's about finding the right person, and I've found my leading lady.' He smiled, just a little, and Zoe's eyes started to sting. 'I just made a stupid error in the casting for a while. Will you forgive me for that? We all make mistakes.'

Zoe found herself nodding as she stared at the rings. Her rings. Or were they Damien's rings? She really didn't know.

Just like that night in the hotel gardens, he pulled her close and kissed her. Zoe didn't even think about slapping him this time. This was what she'd been dreaming about, waiting for, in the long weeks since he'd come to visit her at her workshop. She curled her arms around his neck and kissed him back, gripping the ring box very tightly in one hand.

They finally drew apart and rested their foreheads against each other, their chests rising and falling in rhythm. Damien took her hand and led her towards the far edge of the concrete floor. From there she could see the Thames, grey and pink and glinting yellow in the afternoon sun, snaking its way through the city.

He leaned forward and his breath was deliciously warm in her ear. 'I've fallen in love with a real woman this time, not a perfect creature that doesn't exist.'

She jabbed him in the arm with the ring box. 'Are you saying I'm not perfect?'

He nodded and broke out one of those rare grins that lit up his face. 'Yes. But who is? Not me.'

She pulled him close, using the lapels of his suit for leverage, and kissed him again. 'I think I'm going to need that in writing,' she mumbled against his lips.

Damien laughed and kissed her back, and then he eased the box gently from her fingers, stepped back and got down on one knee. Zoe almost couldn't see him through the tears that had suddenly decided to blur her vision.

'I've never asked anyone this before,' he said, suddenly looking very young. She noticed a little nerve twitching in his left cheek. 'You're the first. The only.'

He took a deep breath and Zoe pressed her palms against her chest, one on top of the other.

'Will you marry me? Because, Zoe St James, I think you are perfect for me.'

'Yes,' she said, her voice sounding faraway and breathless in her own ears. 'Yes, I will.' And she watched in amazement as Damien eased the emerald ring from its cushion and slid it on to her finger. She didn't even notice him stand up, she was so transfixed at the sight of it there.

She laughed softly and then stood on her tiptoes and kissed him again. 'But if you think I'm spending my honeymoon cooped up together on a tiny little yacht with you, going stir-crazy...'

Damien's expression changed to that of an eleven-year-old boy who'd lost his favourite marble. She decided to put him out of his misery.

'You'd be right,' she added with a trademark saucy glimmer in her eye.

# EPILOGUE

ONE year later the little church at St Just-in-Roseland was filled with flowers. No whites or creams for this bride, but a riot of exotic blooms filling the vaulted space with colour and scent.

In the creek outside, a small, recently purchased yacht rocked on the gentle waves, a large white ribbon tied to its bow. It had polished wooden decks and dubious plumbing, but her owners thought she was a dream come true. And, if the wind blew the right way and the boat swung round on her mooring, you could read the freshly painted name plate fixed to her stern—*Sidekick*.

Up in the church, the groom was standing nervously at the head of the aisle, his best friend beside him, and when the organ began to play to announce the entrance of his bride he truly thought his heart had stopped beating.

But then he turned and looked at her, and it started right back up again. Doing a rumba beat.

She was wearing a two-piece gown: a long satin

skirt and a corset, the sort with laces his fingers were already twitching at the thought of undoing, and the bodice was doing something unbelievable to her cleavage.

Okay, heart was definitely working fine again, but now breathing systems were in trouble.

She winked at him as she swayed her way down the aisle. He didn't notice anyone else, not the guests, not the bridesmaid, not even the matron of honour. He felt oxygen swell in his lungs again and he smiled.

Not perfect this bride, not by a long shot. But neither was the groom. And where was the fun in that, anyway? She filled his days with colour and sunshine, and she stopped him becoming old and crusty and grumpy before his time. They fought, of course. Regularly. But making up was so much fun he hardly minded.

She reached him and he decided he couldn't wait: he had to kiss her now, even before the vows had been said and the vicar had given them permission. He leaned in close as she lifted her veil and asked her something softly, so no one else could hear.

'You're not going to slap me if I do, are you?'

She dropped her bouquet, grabbed hold of his

lapels and pulled him close until they were nose to nose, lips only a breath apart. Some of the congregation cheered. The best man stuck his fingers in his mouth and whistled.

'Darling,' she said as she closed her eyes, 'I may slap you if you *don't*.'

* * * * *

Dec 20/13
JC-6
Last Nov 13